## The house still stood there ...

*... a place for cauldrons and witches, with the stink of death. Nancy moved forward into it, up the rotted steps and through the splintered door. The big room was just as she remembered it, the fireplace at the far end. She would need more light, she knew, to examine her surroundings, so she lit a fire with the dried old wood in the fireplace. The flames crackled and in moments the room was alight with the dancing, flickering fire.*

*Nancy glanced around at the walls, seeking some old picture perhaps, some clue to this place. A dust-covered bureau stood against one wall, down at one end because of its broken legs. She pulled open the drawers, looking into each one. But they were all empty.*

*"You won't find anythin'," the voice said.*

*Nancy wheeled around, then saw the firelight glint from the huge blade of a kitchen knife....*

Also by Claudette Nicole

*The Mistress of Orion Hall*
*The Haunting of Drumroe*
*Circle of Secrets*
*The Dark Mill*
*The House at Hawk's End*

# BLOODROOTS MANOR

CLAUDETTE NICOLE

CUTTING EDGE

ISBN-13: 978-1-957868-08-0

Published by
Cutting Edge Books
PO Box 8212
Calabasas, CA 91372
www.cuttingedgebooks.com

# CHAPTER ONE

"THERE MUST BE SOME MISTAKE," Nancy Hazleton said, glancing around quickly, almost fearfully. "There must be some mistake."

But that had become a familiar phrase over the past year, she reminded herself with grim irony. Some of the times she had uttered it she had been right. But the others, the times when there had been no mistake, were seared into her. Still this time she had to be right, she told herself. It had to be a mistake. She turned and half-raised her arm, as if to wave back the train, which was moving off into the dark of the night. But it was nothing more now than a red eye glowing fitfully, mockingly at her in the heavy, humid air. She watched the red eye disappear into the night and turned to look at the old-fashioned, wooden station again. The sign atop the slanted roof of the waiting room said DEEPWELL JUNCTION, all right, as did the smaller sign on the crumbling corner post. The conductor, a thin, nervous man with a high voice, had told her himself, as he put her bags down on the rotted platform, that this was Deepwell Junction. But the waiting room was windowless, boarded shut, and there were dustladen window sills and little squirls of dust in the corners where the wooden supports held the station-house roof. Spider webs clung to every cornice and edged the roof.

Nancy sat down on one of her bags, wiped a bead of perspiration from her short, upturned nose, and fished the little slip of paper from her pocket. The instructions had been sent her in detail and she read them again, squinting in the darkness. She had taken the train one stop past Louisville to a small way station called Harkbell Corners. There, as per the sheet of instructions, she had changed to the little two-car train of the small spur railroad that would carry her into the Little Smokies country and Deepwell Junction. The two-car train had been delayed by mechanical failure; four hours of sitting and waiting for repairs to be made before it chugged on its way again. So, when the conductor nervously put her off she was four hours behind schedule. She could understand not being met, but this silent, dusty, cobwebbed place was absolutely deserted, obviously unused for a long, long time. The soft click-clack of the train wheels had faded away now and only the night sounds remained—the soft buzzing of insects, the sharp sound of the cicadas. And thunder that came with increasing strength each time. The storm had been nearing for the past hour. As she had sat on the almost empty little train, she'd watched the flickering lightning illuminate hills, valleys, thick woods. A flash of lightning came down to brighten the station and herself as though a giant photo-flash had been set off. She glimpsed a road just ahead of her, going past the station and off to the left. A small sign hung on a tree almost directly opposite from where she stood. She walked over and peered up at it. *Oldenhill Road,* it said. Once again, she brought out the slip of instructions.

"From Deepwell Junction, take Oldenhill Road till you reach Cottonwood," she read aloud. "Turn right at Cottonwood till you reach Buckboard. Left on Buckboard Road."

The lightning flashed again and lighted the figure of the girl standing alone, looking so very small and feeling smaller beside the deserted, boarded-up old station. Nancy Hazleton's deep blue eyes nervously looked up at the sky. Her hair, light brown and worn in a short, simple semipageboy, fell loosely around her high-cheekboned face, a sensitive face that was still a little too thin, she kept telling herself. But the determined beauty of it was there, a beauty that was both delicate and strong. The thunder roared again, and Nancy saw that the storm, which had been emitting sharp promises with every passing minute, seemed about to fulfill them. She decided to leave her three bags on the station platform. They would make hurried walking impossible. She could come back for them in the morning.

The girl started to walk along the dirt road. Trees rose up on each side like cliffs of green. She could not shake the feeling that there had been some mistake, that something was wrong, despite the signs on the station and the road. The night had turned cool as the storm approached, and now she hurried to keep warm. The hot, sticky air had given way to sudden coolness that chilled the thin coat of perspiration on her skin. Thunder broke again, bouncing off hills and ridges, echoing back on itself until it sounded like a cannonade. The night was ink-black and surrounded her with a darkness that was almost a physical force. It was a stygian darkness and even though every electric crackle frightened her, she was grateful for the moment of brightness the lightning gave. The road was curving off to the left, she glimpsed, as a flash cracked down over her. She quickened her pace still further. It was so terribly black, so terrifyingly dark, and yet it was something she knew, that total blackness, as only those who have known an inner night can know. It should not frighten her so, anymore, and yet it did. As her mind started to fill with dark thoughts, she spoke to herself, sharply, aloud, with only the trees and the night to hear.

"None of that, Nancy Hazleton," she admonished herself grimly. "You're done with that sort of thing, remember? You've had more than your share of imaginings. That's finished now—over—ended."

The girl straightened up, threw her high, softly rounded breasts out, and marched on, buoyed by her own words. She had to believe them. The past was all too recent. There was not time, yet, to lower one's guard against it. She had learned so much this past year, hard things, terrible things, but they were

3

things that could make her stronger for the knowing. Most people never came to learn that dreams could be as real as reality itself, that the mind could build worlds of its own and imprison you in them. Most young girls never knew that shock and terror were the ghosts of the soul, capable of haunting the mind, of twisting and turning the senses. These things she knew, now, and at the hospital they had told her that knowing was strength not weakness, good not bad. And later, during the long months of putting her shattered self back together, she had realized that she indeed did have an inner core of steely strength. That, and the satisfaction of knowing she had been more right than wrong, that her emotions had not lied to her, had pulled her through. But it hadn't stopped the hurt or less-ened the impact.

Another flash split the blackness, just as she drew abreast of a small road breaking the line of trees on both sides. Her eyes caught the weathered sign on the tree: *Cottonwood Road.* She turned right on Cottonwood Road and found herself on a narrow path where the trees bent inwards, reaching out to touch her as she brushed past them. She saw twin pinpoints of light in front of her as lightning flashed in the sky again. They became an opos-sum carrying a smaller animal in its jaws. The creature glared at her and ran into the trees. Nancy stopped, drew a deep breath, and forced herself to go on. Why, oh why, hadn't the station been a warm, lighted, cozy place where she could have waited till someone finally came to pick her up? She hurried on, brushing past leaves cold and wet with dew. She shrank back momentarily as a spider web brushed against her forehead, and she swept it away with one hand. She almost ran into the sign at eye level on the trunk of the beechwood tree. *Buckboard Road,* it said and an arrow on it pointed left.

Nancy turned, following the arrow, and found the road even narrower, more uneven and the trees hanging lower made her bend over as she hurried. She felt her legs brush and knock against sharp branches and once more she thought, there must be some mistake.

Then, with startling suddenness, the path opened and she stood very still to stare up at the huge, dark bulk of the house that loomed up in front of her, surrounded on all sides by trees that crowded in on it and pressed down. A lightning flash opened the night and Nancy heard herself gasp. The house before her was a monstrous, shattered, and shuttered derelict of a place, gabled ends sagging like the broken wings of a vulture. She saw a bat fly from one black hole in the corner of the roof. The lightning flash disappeared and the huge, black bulk stood there in front of her, menacing, ominous. Lightning flashes again let her see the scars of age that had cracked open one end of the house. It was a withered, gaping, toothless, old crone of a place, terrifying to behold, that seemed to cackle and dare one to look upon its ugliness. The front columns leaned into each other under the sagging roofline, and now, again, Nancy knew there had been a mistake of some kind. Either she had made it, taken a wrong turn someplace, or the conductor had let her off at the wrong place, despite the signs on the station. She was sure of that, or of the fact that this couldn't be the house she'd come down to redesign. Only bats and field mice lived in this hulk of a house, this ancient relic that the forest had gathered to itself.

The girl was about to try and trace her way back when the storm broke, striking with a wild fury of pelting rain carried by a cold wind. Thunder crashed and the lightning struck close. Nancy felt herself cry out, felt the rain beating down at her with the force of an ocean wave. She ran forward, up the broken steps of the house, stumbling and catching herself as one gave way under her. The rain pursued her, slamming into her. In a few seconds she was nearly soaked to the skin with the force of the downpour. The house would at least be a kind of refuge and dry. She pushed against the door and it fell in with a splintering sound, and she stood inside what was once a living room. During the lightning flashes she saw bits and pieces of rotted wooden chairs and tables. There was a big fireplace at the far end of the room and she crossed toward it, skirting the debris inside the room. She sniffed and caught that strange, inimitable odor that rotting houses have, made up of dryness and dampness, peeled wallpaper and moldy fabric, the smell of things forgotten and deserted.

She shivered, her wet dress clinging to her skin. She dipped into the pockets of her dress. She always carried matches. She had been an inveterate matchbox collector for years. There was no need of paper to start a fire. The wood was so old and dry it would surely burn at once. She picked up a few pieces and tossed them into the fireplace. It might smoke, but anything would be better than catching pneumonia in a soaked dress. She lighted a few matches, placed them against the wood, and stepped back. The yellow-tipped flame caught at once, and the wood began to burn with a crackling, popping sound. Thunder shook the old house and the roof sagged and creaked. The rain slashed in through the broken windows and the wind blew against her and she shivered. Nancy threw on more wood, half of an old chair, and the fire leaped up. There was plenty of draw to the chimney, and the flames sent out their warming shafts. Nancy stood before the fire, turning her body around in front of it, letting the warmth dry her dress. Finally, she sat down in front of it, cross-legged, and huddled by its warmth as outside the storm raged and beat down with its thunderous onslaught of wind and rain. Nancy let her eyes watch the dancing flames and she began to relax enough to think back on what had brought her here to this nightmare.

She had moved back into her apartment after leaving the hospital and her convalescence at Aunt Edna's place. She finished the last three months she had left to go at the Academy of Interior Design and had just graduated when the telephone call came that night, a Friday night, she recalled so clearly. Long distance, from Deepwell Junction, Kentucky. The caller identified himself at once in a clear, deep voice as Samuel Howell. He had contacted the school, he said, and they had given him her name, along with a few others. It had been an excitingly unexpected call that grew more so with each passing minute. He wanted her to contract to come down to his house in the Little Smokies region of the Kentucky hills and redesign the entire interior.

"I want you to stay here with us, get the feel of the place, live here, study it," he'd said. "You can do your work right here with us."

She had tried to contain the excitement that had leaped inside her. Her first job. A real, honest-to-goodness assignment. An entire house to redesign. It was almost unbelievable. Samuel Howell had gone on about travel expenses and a hundred dollar advance fee to bind the agreement. She had hardly heard him for the excited thoughts racing through her head.

"We're in the very deepest part of the Little Smokies, around Ten Men Mountain," he had said. "But I don't suppose you've ever heard of that. We're outside the mainstream of the world, been so for more'n a hundred years and we like it that way. But my daughter, Jodie, she wants the place redone and I guess I have to give in."

He went on and Nancy quickly agreed that she was indeed interested. There was more talk of his sending her written instructions and details of her arrival, and when she'd hung up she was happy, really happy, for the first time in too long to remember. "I guess it's time I had something good happen to me," she had said simply, and now, before the fire, she recalled how Samuel Howell's letter of detailed instructions and a check had arrived a few days later. The letter had told her the name of the place, *Bloodroots Manor,* and she remembered how she had thought it a rather odd, gruesome name. But she had, of course, checked things out with the Academy. They had confirmed Samuel Howell's call to them and so she'd gathered her things and taken the train, happy, excited, thrilled. Now, in this frightening old house, huddled from the storm, she was again certain there had been some mistake, either on her part or on that of the conductor. Had she taken the wrong little train after she left the big streamliner that one stop past Louisville? Perhaps there was another Deepwell Junction, not even in Kentucky, and that's where she'd gotten off.

A dark shadow crossed her mind and she angrily flung it aside. When the storm stopped she would find her way back to the deserted station and walk along the tracks till she came to a place where she could get information. There would be, she'd learn, a reasonable, perfectly plausible explanation to it all. There always was, even when it shattered the mind, she heard herself say silently. She shivered, got up, and threw a round, thick table leg on the fire. Sitting down again, she stared into the fire, not daring to look at the shapes it threw upon the sagging old walls. The thunder had slackened but the rain still pelted the roof and dripped down through the holes at the corners of the house. But beside the fire it was warm, and her dress dried out quickly. The wind had died down, too, and the rain had calmed to a steady tattoo on the roof. The girl had no idea how long she'd been sitting huddled before the fire when she felt her skin suddenly start to crawl, to grow cold despite the fire's heat. She sat very still and with the instinctive sense still left from the primordial, that instinct that passes knowledge, she knew she was not alone.

Fear clutched at her heart, sudden, instinctive fear. Still facing the fire, Nancy moved slowly, getting to one knee, then to her feet. Only then did she turn to the doorway. Something stood there, a dark shape. The shape moved forward and the firelight caught it. The girl's body froze, her heart turning to ice. Her throat tightened in parched dryness and the scream she sought refused to come. The figure before her stood still, black hair flowing wildly from its head, a face that had surely been summoned from some witch's cauldron. A glob of flesh with an ugly scar of a mouth, twisted and hanging at one end, eyes that flamed with a demoniac fire, like that of a mad stallion with the whites fully exposed. It was a creature that seemed to have stepped out of the depths of some primeval ooze, human yet not human, something from a nightmare's deepest horrors. But it was no nightmare. It was there, in front of her. Nancy closed her eyes tightly and pulled them open again. It was still there. And then, as if to dispel her self-doubts, it moved forward with a shuffle—swaying, apelike, and small guttural sounds burbled from its throat. She saw it had on trousers, bare feet sticking out at the ends of them, and a tattered shirt. But it was the eyes that fascinated the girl— wild, rolling and casting about, yet piercing. Then, with surprising quickness, the creature leaped forward in a long bound.

Nancy found the scream and it tore from her throat. Yet she heard it as though it came from far away. A long arm reached out for her. She twisted away, but a hand caught the front of her dress. She pulled and heard the dress rip away. The creature moved fast as she broke away again and tried to run. It moved to block her path, and she saw the mouth opening and closing in rapid, chewing movements as it devoured air. This time she wasn't fast enough as an arm caught her waist, ripping off the rest of the top of her dress. A hand closed around her mouth, and she saw the huge, purple strawberry-shaped mark on it, just back of the thumb. She clamped her teeth down on the choking, suffocating hand, biting down as hard as she could. The creature cried out in pain and the hand drew away. She tore from its grip. It could feel pain, at least. It reached for her again and she ducked, twisting away and under the long, grasping arm. But now she was backing against the fireplace and she saw the creature start toward her, its Neanderthal sounds holding a kind of triumph. Nancy reached into the fire, seizing one end of the table leg, steeling herself against the burning heat of it on her hand. She yanked it from the fire and whirled, thrusting it into the creature's demoniac face, feeling sick and nauseated as she did so. The thing screamed in pain and backed away, a scream that shook the house, and Nancy's stomach turned at the odor of charred flesh. As it clapped both hands to its face, Nancy ran past, the rest of her torn dress falling from her, and she was a milk-white wraith in bra and panties racing into the rain.

She ran headlong into the woods, ignoring the rain that struck at her, soaking her instantly, and the sharp branches that slapped at her body. Behind her the creature had stopped its cry of pain and now bellowed in a gargantuan rage. She heard the heavy thud of it coming after her. As lightning flashed, she glanced back and saw the dark shape stop, draw back and cower. The lightning obviously frightened it, but she wasn't waiting to observe with scientific detachment. She flew through the woods, slamming into small trees, falling, getting up and running in any direction, any way, but running. The thing was following, she could hear. She had to keep ahead of it. She raced through the thick woods, heedless of the fact that her legs and feet were torn and bleeding. In another bright flash of lightning she glimpsed the dark shape behind her, saw it again stop and cower, and she prayed for more lightning. With every flash it fell a little farther behind in its pursuit. It seemed to be confused, its bellowing more aimless now. Nancy found herself on a sharp incline and she raced down it, falling on wet leaves underfoot, rolling, struggling to her feet and running on, trying to grab at tree branches to slow her descent. The storm was tapering off, the rain coming to an end, and the temperature ten degrees colder. But Nancy didn't notice nor care. Blind fear drove her onward, but her body was beginning to give out. Her legs were leaden weights now, and she felt her strength slipping away. She fell against a broad tree trunk and paused for breath that burned in her chest as she swallowed.

Was the creature still following? She didn't know. She was almost beyond hearing, feeling, knowing. She forced herself onward and suddenly, with a steep drop, the incline ended and she felt herself falling. She landed hard, glimpsed a small road.

Was there a light across it, on the other side, a window? Her eyes refused to obey her command to see, her body refused her command to rise. The world was spinning, spinning, spinning away on its own, leaving her behind. A dreadful, all-consuming exhaustion was upon her.

"Help me," she heard herself cry out. "Oh, God, please somebody help me." She put her head down on the wet ground, sobs wracking her body. How often had she cried out those words, she knew. It seemed so much of her vocabulary was torn from the past. Nancy lay there, unable to move, her body wracked and shaking with silent, gulping sobs. The last of the rain swept over her near-naked form. The trees tossed a handful of leaves down on her bloodied and mud-soaked loveliness. She neither saw nor heard the door of the cabin open on the other side of the road. The flashlight that swept the darkness did not reach her still form. The young man under the leather poncho walked out a few feet, listening for the sound, the sound that had seemed like a cry. He moved the flashlight over the road and its beam picked out the girl's crumpled form. Nancy did not wake as she was picked up and carried into the cabin.

# CHAPTER TWO

NANCY DID NOT OPEN HER EYES till morning and then, before she opened them, before she saw the sun had warmed the land in clear, bright colors, the horrible creature leaped up in her mind again. The old house and the horror of the night caught at her and she sat up with a cry, her heart pounding. She found herself looking with fear-filled eyes at a young man sitting in a heavy, wood chair, gazing into eyes that were hazel, soft, and warm.

"Good morning," he said and his smile was slow, easy. She looked around and saw she was in a large cabin. Glancing down at herself, she saw she had on a shirt of red wool, much too big for her. She could feel that her body, lost in the enveloping folds of the shirt, was naked underneath. She was on a bed against one wall of the cabin, a blanket covering the rest of her. Her eyes went back to the young man. A tape recorder sat on a table in front of him and stacks of boxes lined the far wall. He got up and she noticed that he had sandy hair over a thin, pleasant face on a tall, rangy body. A pipe jutted from the pocket of his open-necked shirt. Only as her eyes swept the rest of the cabin did she see the other figure sitting in the open doorway, a young boy, it seemed, with unruly blond hair falling over one eye, a guitar across his lap. He was looking in at her, and she thought she saw a secretive smile playing around his lips.

"How do you feel?" the tall young man asked, putting a hand on her forehead. "No fever," he said. "You'll be all right. What's left of your underclothes have dried out by now."

There was a small pinpoint of light dancing in his hazel eyes, and she felt her cheeks redden. "Did you find me?" she asked, her voice soft, faint.

"Yes," he said. "Jed came by just a few minutes ago. The pleasure was all mine."

She looked up at him but the laughter in his eyes held no bite and a sudden, surprisingly wanton pleasure gathered inside her. Dirk had been the only man who had ever seen her completely nude before this. Dirk! It was the first time she'd uttered the name, even to herself, since that last night. It was funny she should do so now, because another man had undressed her, bathed, and tended to her. It was as funny as the fact that she felt no embarrassment, only a secret pleasure he had found her worth looking at.

"I'm glad you enjoyed it," she said, meeting his eyes, her head lifting in a characteristic gesture of pride.

"Couldn't deny it," he said. "I'm Peter Thatcher." He gestured to the figure in the doorway. "And that's Jed Batterbee."

"I'm Nancy Hazleton," the girl said and she saw the young man's eyes grow serious.

"You were in pretty bad shape," he said. "Full of cuts and bruises. The only time you half woke you were delirious. What in God's name happened to you? How'd you get out there in that condition?"

"I don't really know myself," she said solemnly. "That is, I know but I don't understand any of it. And I wouldn't expect you to believe me. I wouldn't believe it myself if I hadn't gone through it."

"Try me," he said, sitting down on the edge of the bed and putting the unlighted pipe into his mouth. "I'll be honest with you when you're finished."

Nancy hesitated, knowing how perfectly ridiculous it would all sound, and suddenly unwilling to even want to recall the horrors of the night. But she had to recall it, she knew, and she took a deep breath and began.

"I was engaged to come down and redesign the interior of a house around here," she said. "It belongs to Mr. Samuel Howell and they call it Bloodroots Manor."

"Yes, I know the place," Peter Thatcher said. "Everyone in these hills knows of Bloodroots and the Howells. They're the power family here. It's just off Buckboard Road."

"Yes, I found it," Nancy said, her eyes wide. "But it's a total wreck, an abandoned apparition, a monstrosity."

"Bloodroots?" Peter Thatcher frowned. "I don't know about it being the last word in interior design but it's far from an abandoned apparition. It's very big and opulent, a little too heavy and forbidding for my tastes, but very impressive."

"But it can't be," Nancy said. "The house I came to off Buckboard Road was a derelict, in the middle of the woods."

"Maybe you'd better start over again, Nancy," Peter Thatcher said.

"Mister Pete." It was the young boy in the doorway, on his feet now. "I'm going strolling. Be back later."

"Don't forget to come back," Peter said. "I want to finish that last tape."

The boy smiled at Nancy and she saw that he was not really a boy at all and not really a man, either. His face was smooth-cheeked as a girl's, his body slender as hers, with a lithe, supple quality to it and his face had a fey, elfin cast to its smooth features. The small smile that clung to his lips had that same, fey, secretive air to it. He left with a chord from the guitar, a musical good-bye and was out of sight instantly. Nancy turned back to see Peter Thatcher's eyes studying her.

"All right, I'll start again," she said grimly. "I followed the instructions given me and got off the train at Deepwell Junction. There's no question about that. The sign said so. Is there another Deepwell Junction anywhere around here?"

"No," Peter said. "Not that I've ever heard of, anyway."

"Well, this place was closed down tight, boarded up, cob-webbed and dust-covered. There wasn't even a light."

"What did the waiting room look like?" Peter asked.

"Long, low-roofed, with a broken corner post at the right corner."

"Go on," Peter Thatcher said quietly. Nancy hurried on with her story, telling him of walking up Oldenhill Road, then onto Cottonwood, turning on Buckboard.

"That's the way to Bloodroots Manor, all right," he commented as she went on. But he said nothing again till she had finished her story, her breath coming in harsh, shallow draughts and her body trembling. He put a hand on her shoulder and the trembling lessened. "Take it easy," he said quietly. He disappeared into a small side room and appeared a few minutes later with a cup of hot tea. He sat down on the chair and watched her sip it.

"That has to be one of the wildest, weirdest stories ever heard," he said finally.

"But it's true, it happened, every word of it," Nancy cried out, and she felt herself blanch at her own words, familiar words again, the past leaping into the present again. She took a long drink of the hot tea to still the frightened wildness that threatened to engulf her.

"Nancy Hazleton," she heard Peter Thatcher say and she was grateful for the gentleness in his voice. "Lots of times things seem real when they aren't."

Nancy closed her eyes and wished she could close her ears. Good Lord, how often had she heard those words before. She grimaced as she opened her eyes, almost angrily. Almost, but not quite. Memory held back anger. Fear dragged on pride.

"If I made it all up, how did I get into the condition you found me in?" she glared at Peter Thatcher, at his soft, steady hazel eyes. "Or did I imagine my own cuts and bruises? They're very real, I believe. You saw them yourself."

"They're real," Peter smiled quietly. "And you were in a state of total shock when I found you. And your description of the railroad station is perfect, except that it's a perfect description of the old Deepwell Junction station that hasn't been used in twenty-five years, not since the new station was built on the main track line. The old station is on the old spur line that hasn't been used either for twenty-five years. And your description of how to reach Bloodroots Manor was perfect, too. Of course, I can only guess about what really happened to you."

"Suppose you guess out loud," Nancy snapped. "I'd like to hear what happened to me." She didn't mean to sound so bitingly sarcastic and was glad Peter Thatcher only smiled at her.

"All right, let's have a go at it," he said genially. "You got off at the station, the right one, not the old one. You were hours late you said, so no one was there to meet you. It was dark and late and you started walking. You got lost. The storm hit and made matters worse. You began to panic, tried to retrace your steps to the station but you grew even more lost. Panic really set in then. The storm, the lightning turned the woods into a thousand strange shapes. The rest was merely a matter of your mind taking off, panicked by fear and terror. The mind can do things, once set off, that defy reasoned explanation. You suffered an acute case of fright and terror with the results that come with that sort of thing."

"Very rational," Nancy sniffed. "And very wrong. I didn't go back to any old station. I got off at it. I looked at the big sign over the boarded-up waiting room roof and the little one on the corner post. Then I followed the signs on the roads."

"Nancy," Peter said, patience in his voice. "There aren't any signs on the old station. I've been there. I know. They were taken down twenty years ago, I'd wager."

"There were signs," Nancy shouted. "There were signs. And there was that terrible old house and that, that... sub-human creature."

"Trying to convince yourself?" he said quietly. "Dreams can be terribly powerful, Nancy. Imagination can be real."

"Oh, God, I know that all too well!" Nancy exploded and saw his eyebrows lift. She bit her tongue, furious at her slip, but she didn't amplify the remark, letting it go without further comment.

"Can you take me to Bloodroots Manor?" she asked quietly.

"My pleasure," Peter said. "I've an old pair of dungarees you can put on. I'll get them and your underthings."

She swung her long, slender legs over the edge of the bed, making certain the long shirt covered most of her and stepped down onto the floor. She noted the cuts and bruises on her legs with distaste. She walked to Peter Thatcher, put a hand on his arm, and looked up at his soft eyes. He was even taller than he seemed when she was on the bed.

"I'm really very grateful to you," she said. "I could have died out there, I know."

"Possibly," he agreed. "But you didn't, and I'm glad about that. Perhaps sometime you might explain that last rather cryptic statement of yours."

Nancy's eyes darkened and she knew well which one he meant. "Sometime, maybe," she said. "I guess I owe you that much, at least."

He left, went into the little area off the one large room, returned with her bra and panties. Drawing a burlap curtain beside the bed, he let her change behind it and when she was finished she drew back the curtain and stepped out in the voluminous red shirt and the wide, baggy dungarees. Peter Thatcher laughed.

"The mark of a really pretty girl," he said. "One who can look good in any old thing. Or nothing."

Nancy laughed at the little glint in his eyes. "Thank you, kind sir," she said. "Peter, what do you do here? Is this your home?"

"No, no, I'm strictly an outsider," he said. "What the folks around here call an outlander. I'm here on a grant from the state university. Actually I'm a sociologist. I've been here for almost a year, tracing the history and migration of the people of this region. There is no record of them, officially, at least. They just exist here, in this backwater of our country. It's almost a lost land of its own. It's been tucked away for hundreds of years, the people keeping to their own ways with their own customs. They're the purest collection of inbred families I've ever encountered in any hill people anywhere."

"Are you getting anywhere with it?" Nancy asked.

"It's damned slow and difficult," Peter said. "Having an official status hasn't done much except stop them from running me out as they would any ordinary snooper. But I learn from the little things I piece together." He turned and reached into a corner, holding up a guitar very much like the one the young man Jed had held in his lap.

"This has been my surprise investigative tool," he said. "It's something I would never have thought of but it's been absolutely amazing."

"A guitar?"

"Yes, but really what it means. Music, Nancy, music. The history of these people is written in their folk songs. It's all there, in the story-song form of folk music. The music tells us where they have come from. The words they've written tell us of their past here. And the newer music, that they've added in the last hundred years, tells us more things. It's easy enough to take a nose count of the families alive here now. It's their past, their origins and history, that the music reveals. For example, many of their songs are almost note for note those of Elizabethan ballads."

"Which means they come fron English stock," Nancy commented.

"Exactly," Peter said. "And some of the music of their hill songs is music still sung in Ireland, ancient Celtic music. So by using tapes and recording, they show me their origins. And some of them have even gotten to talk to me, a little anyway. Each one says something and I put it together with what someone else said about a time, event, or a place. Slowly, I build up a record. I've even gotten quite accurate family genealogies on some clans, all from little snips and bits."

Peter's hand on her arm guided her out and around to the back of the cabin. It looked more substantial from inside than from outside. Against the right side, she saw an ancient open-topped car. She recognized it as an old Model A Ford, drawing a surprised comment from Peter by it.

"My uncle used to be a bug on cars, vintage ones," she said. "As he and my aunt Edna raised me, I got to learn them by sight."

Nancy climbed into the front seat with Peter and they were about to drive off when Jed Batterbee appeared. The boy came over, his tousled blond hair falling loosely, and Nancy saw again that his was an ageless face, young and old, innocent and wise, a pixie and a sage. His eyes, a light, light blue, almost washed out in their lightness, surveyed her, and the small smile of secret wisdom withheld played around his lips. He took the guitar from around his shoulders and strummed a chord on it.

> "Wish I was, a red, rosey bush,
>   On the banks of the sea,
> Everytime, my true love walked past,
>   She'd pick a rose, off of me...."

He sang the little verse in a light, clear voice, softly musical and pleasant.

"That's Jed's way of telling you he likes you," Peter said, and Nancy felt a rush of warmth for this strange, fey boy. Or man. Or whatever he was.

"Thank you, Jed," Nancy said. Jed Batterbee said nothing but the small smile seemed to grow the tiniest bit deeper. Or did she just imagine so.

"Be back in a few minutes, Jed. Wait for me?" Jed nodded and turned to the cabin as they drove off.

"He's a strange person, isn't he?" Nancy said to Peter. "How old is Jed?"

Peter laughed. "Good question. I wish I knew the answer. Old enough, is what he told me once when I asked. I've gathered enough to know that he's a lot older than he looks. He's the troubadour of the Little Smokies and especially this valley behind Ten Men Mountain. He seldom speaks but he sings his words, wrapping everything he wants to say in a song. And it's a lifetime characteristic I've found invaluable. He's been a gold mine of information to me. He's a walking storehouse of every piece of music, every ballad, every verse, every bit of folk song ever sung or heard in this part of the country. His songs have put together more bits and pieces for me than I can count. But Jed has to be handled right. No pushing. He'll parcel things out in his own way and his own time."

Nancy hesitated, trying to phrase her next question at least with good taste. "He seems, well, *different* in a strange sort of way," she said. "Or perhaps I've just never met anyone quite like him."

"I'm sure you haven't," Peter said and she saw him grinning at her. "But I understand what you're asking. Jed's a product of this country, of inwardly turned family units that never marry outside their clan, of inbreeding and of incest, of all the things which biologists say you should never do. Not that they aren't right. But here in the Little Smokies they've been doing it for hundreds of years. This place is a biologist's paradise, too. But to get back to Jed. Is he simple? Yes, and then no. Many of these people are really retarded, showing the results of their generations of inbreeding and incest. Jed Batterbee is a child of some strange combination of genetic forces. He's simple, yet I always feel he possesses a secret kind of wisdom denied to others, ordinary people such as you and I. He's part throwback to the madrigal singers of the Middle Ages, part genetic aberration, part lost soul, part human, and part elf, I sometimes think."

Nancy laughed and forced herself to look away from Peter Thatcher's long, kind face. There was a gentleness in it that lay over a strength. It was a reassuring face, not handsome but something better, a face with character to it. She'd had enough of the power of handsomeness, she said silently. The land they drove through was full of rolling dips and gulleys and ridges, and it was all thickly green with dense woods. Here and there she saw a rundown house, smoke curling from a chimney. They made a sharp turn and Nancy saw the railroad station at the very bottom of a hill, a long diesel train rushing past it. The road paralleled the station, on a higher level, and as Peter turned onto another connecting road she saw the sign, *Oldenhill Road.* It was the same sign she had seen last night. Or it certainly looked the same. But she said nothing and watched as they drove on in silence. Finally Peter turned the old car to the right, onto another road, and her eyes took in the sign, *Cottonwood Road.* But these weren't narrow paths hardly wide enough for her body. These were country roads, dirt and dust, but wide enough for two cars or two wagons. When she saw the weathered sign that read *Buckboard Road,* Peter swung left and her heart had heavy weights tied onto it now. They drove up a small incline and suddenly, ahead of her, she saw the big house, towering, thick columns of white gracing the entranceway. Heavy wooden frames surrounded the windows and the roof curved outward from the top, bringing the gables forward to give the house the appearance of wearing a shawl. But the house was well kept. This was not the terrible derelict of a gaping old house she had met last night. But even more impressive than the house were the two lawns of flowers that swept up to the front of the house, thousands and thousands of star-pointed cream-white flowers, glistening in the sun against leaves of soft gray-green underneath them. They formed a carpet of soft white that swept to the front of the house on both sides of the stone driveway that led to the entrance.

"Bloodroots Manor," Peter said softly to her.

"How beautiful," Nancy breathed. "How did they ever get that name?"

"Inside the roots and stems is a reddish sap," he answered. "Roots of blood. Or so someone once thought. But they are beautiful, aren't they?"

They were almost at the entranceway and she turned to Peter, her hand touching his arm. "Will you promise to do something for me?" she asked quickly. "I know you purposely drove near the main station of the railroad just now back there so I could see it. But will you drive me to the old station? I'll prove to you I'm right about what I said."

His eyes were serious and he gave a small shrug. "Of course," he said. "Tomorrow, if you'd like."

"I'd like," she said. "Everything I told you about happened. The station, the signs, the old house, that terrible creature, *everything!*"

His eyes were studying her. "We'll talk more about it," was all he said. Nancy looked away, her fists clenched, feeling her fingernails dig deeply into her skin, the way they used to do. She opened her hands. Damn the past, she said silently. Damn yesterday. Damn Dirk and his handsomeness. That was the second time she'd mentioned his name to herself within the hour. They'd told her at the hospital that it was all right to look back in anger, in hate. She snorted. She was doing just that.

But the question marks hung there in the spaces of her mind, and she couldn't look past them. She trembled for a moment, like a leaf that feels the tug of the wind on its secure branch.

# CHAPTER THREE

THE MAN FILLED THE ENTRANCEWAY almost completely as he strolled out, his huge body clothed in a white linen suit. His hair, brown tinged with gray, sat atop a florid face that was all folds and jowls with sharp blue eyes peering out from the mass of skin. The girl that came out behind him, Nancy quickly noted, was all curves and sensual, rounded lines, large, deep breasts ballooning from a white cotton blouse. She wore blue hip-huggers that accentuated her wide, seductive hips. But her eyes made Nancy's voice catch in her throat. Only once before had she seen eyes so deep and dark as those, so liquid and intense that they seemed to have their own, dark light inside them. God, but this was her morning to think of Dirk, Nancy swore under her breath. Nancy stepped from the old car as it came to a halt, and saw the girl give Peter a dazzling smile that was purely and solely for him.

"Howdy, folks," Peter said easily, swinging from the car. "This is the young lady you've been expecting, I hear."

Samuel Howell's voice was as booming as he was big, and he turned and enveloped Nancy with a huge arm around her. "Why, my goodness, we'd wondered what happened to you, child," he said. "We kept making trips down to the station until we found out the train had been delayed for hours. Then that rip-roaring storm came up and the roads turned to mud and we had to stay put here."

"Miss Hazleton took a wrong turn somewhere, got caught in the storm and tried to run. I think she must have been hit by a branch or possibly even knocked unconscious by lightning. In any case, she wandered around in a daze, and I found her on the road outside my place all cut and in a state of total shock."

"Well, then, we're mighty beholdin' to you, Mr. Thatcher," Samuel Howell said, giving Nancy a broad smile, his deep face shaking with every movement. Nancy uttered a silent amen to his words. Peter hadn't believed a word of her story but he had smoothly and easily supplied her with one he felt would be believed. She'd express her appreciation at their next meeting. Samuel Howell turned to the girl, who was busy sidling up to Peter. "This is my daughter, Jodie," he boomed out. Jodie Howell turned those black-brown liquid eyes on Nancy, who felt her heart flip over in bitter memory.

"The stationmaster had your suitcases delivered to us," she said. "They're in your room." She smiled but Nancy sensed there was really no smile in her, not for her anyway. Another figure came out of the house, an older girl, this one all angles and sharp lines, as tall as Jodie, but a stone opposite a flame.

"And this here's my other daughter, Cassie," Samuel Howell introduced Nancy. Cassie nodded and smiled a hard, mechanical smile. Hers at least fit her face. Jodie's had had a strange hidden something in it.

"I'm sorry I messed things up so," Nancy said to Samuel Howell. The huge man only laughed a deep, roaring laugh.

"I'm sorry you had such a poor introduction to our Little Smokies," he said. He should know, Nancy added to herself. "But we'll make things comfortable for you now," he went on.

He guided her into the house. Nancy turned to catch Peter's eye and saw Jodie walking down the path with him, her arm linked in his. Samuel Howell stopped at the door of the big living room, and Nancy brought her attention back to him. The room was huge, a row of large windows on one wall. It was old, worn, unrealized, a room with a thousand possibilities for her, and her creative enthusiasm skyrocketed.

"What do you think, Nancy, girl?" Samuel Howell asked.

"I think wonders can be done with it," she said happily. She'd forgotten why she'd come here with the terrors of the night, but now she felt the excitement of her creative spirit taking hold to seize her in its magical grip.

"Well, you have all the time you want to do whatever you like with it," Samuel Howell said. He guided Nancy from the room to the foot of a graceful winding staircase of polished cherry. He paused as a gaunt-faced man shuffled into the room, stooped but still tall for all his round-shoulderedness.

"This here is Zachary," Samuel Howell said. "Zachary's the best handyman in the valley. Anything you want, you just ask Zachary, you hear?"

Nancy nodded and noted that Zachary's eyes were small dots of flat, expressionless gray in his gaunt face. Just then Jodie came back into the house with Cassie following her. The older sister was, Nancy saw, not very different in actual size from Jodie. It was just that everything she had was shaped differently and her body seemed a thing of flat planes instead of soft curves. Where Jodie's breasts were round and full and sensuous, Cassie's were big and shapeless. Where Jodie's hips curved in rounded lines, Cassie's stuck out like a clothes hanger.

"I'll show Miss Hazleton to her room, Pa," Jodie said, and she started up the stairway.

"Please call me Nancy," Nancy said and followed her up the heavy, wide steps. Jodie exuded a raw, primitive sexuality with every movement, Nancy saw as she followed up the stairs. At the first floor landing, Jodie walked a few feet down the hallway to the first room. Nancy glanced on down the hall and saw the corridor grow dark at the rear of the house. Two old chairs were wedged against a closed door at the very end of the hall. The rest of the stairway wound up to the second or attic floor and Nancy saw Jodie watching her from the doorway of the room.

"We never go upstairs," Jodie said. "Anyway, it's the main part of the house you'll be concerned with, downstairs. And maybe my room and Cassie's in the east wing." Nancy wondered if Jodie's remarks were more than an idle comment. The girl had something unsaid about her, as if she were really two people. "Pa says you're to have anything you want," she said. It was there again, Nancy noted. Sometimes the girl sounded quite sophisticated and other times, when she spoke of her father, she lapsed into a hillbilly drawl and nasality. Nancy walked into the room and saw it was bright and spacious. Two big windows looked out over the hills and ridges. She turned at a sound and saw Zachary in the doorway. The gaunt-faced man paused and went on and Jodie opened a doorway at one end of the room. She gestured to the bathroom with unabashed pride.

"Bloodroots is about the only house in the valley that's got an indoor bathroom," she said. "We've got two. One here and one by Pa's room on the other side of the house."

Jodie Howell's deep, liquid eyes turned fully on Nancy, and Nancy again felt the sharp spear of memory. God, she seemed to be doomed to be haunted by Dirk, she said angrily to herself. The girl even had the same slightly arrogant tilt to her chin. Dammit, why couldn't she have had green eyes or blue or gray. But then, she remembered, she used to see those black brown, liquid eyes on a lot of faces for a long time. Maybe it was still just that and no more. But she looked at Jodie and knew differently. The girl just had the same kind of eyes and she'd have to live with it until her job here was finished. Perhaps it was just one more challenge thrown her way to overcome. One more wouldn't hurt now.

"I'll change out of these things and be down to look around some more," Nancy said. She paused but Jodie made no move to leave. Nancy took the voluminous red shirt off and then stepped out of the baggy trousers, conscious of Jodie's eyes on her. She stood straight, glad for the smooth slender loveliness of her figure and her own high breasts, beautifully shaped and pointed. Jodie's look seemed to carry a silent evaluation, a hidden meaning wrapped in an appraisal. Nancy wondered about it as the girl finally turned and walked from the room. Alone in the room, Nancy closed the door and saw, with a strange sense of relief, that there was a bolt on it. She folded Peter's clothes and put them neatly on a chair. The bed was firm and wide, a double bed with four high posts at each corner. She went into the bathroom, washed, and then put on a simple dress of light blue, a shirtwaist that was neat yet stylish. She went to the windows and gazed out. They didn't look over the white carpet of bloodroots in the front of the house but her view took in one side and the land as it dipped and rose in ridges of thick green. There was a lawn of thick green stretching up to a ridge, the line of the woods bordering it at the far side, going right up and over the ridge. Her body still hurt and she decided to stretch out on the bed for ten minutes. It was a trick she'd garnered long ago, a breather, a refresher, and it usually worked.

This time it didn't. Her mind kept returning to the nightmare that was the night before. It burned into her, but not so much for what had happened. It was what it meant that frightened her even more. It happened, she had told Peter Thatcher. It happened, she knew inside herself. But what if it hadn't? In any case, it wouldn't have been the way Peter Thatcher had rationalized it, she knew. If it hadn't happened, then the past was not past. She got to her feet and started to unpack her clothes, her hands trembling as she hung them in the big, walk-in closet. Keeping herself physically busy had always helped. It had been a way of forgetting endless nights of crying, of tortured fears, and later, of doctors and therapists and long sessions of unresolved talking. And now, suddenly, it was all flooding back on her again. Last night brought it all back. Fearful as it was, terrifying as it had been, she fervently wished it to have been real. But at the hospital they had told her that unusual nervousness, stress, and strain could trigger problems. Had she been that wound up about the job, her first real opportunity? Had she been that tensed with nerves over it all? It was possible, she knew, and she closed her eyes in anguish. No, she told herself again. It happened. It all happened. That monstrous creature was real.

She took her big sketch pad and some pencils and flew out of the door. Working was the best thing. It always chased away the darkness. It was a weapon only the creative had, and she thanked God for it.

Samuel Howell was in the living room, in a big easy chair. As she entered, he started to rise. "Please, don't," Nancy said quickly. "I'll come back. I was only going to make some sketches."

"No, no, you go right ahead, my dear," he said in his deep, resonant voice. "You forget that I'm even here. While you're here you are one of us. In fact, you really are, you know. Here in Deepwell Valley there's not too much to do. We live by ourselves and make our own world. That's the way the folks in the valley want it. We feud and we fight sometimes, but it's all kept here within our valley. But we can talk more about this country at dinner. You get on with your sketching."

Nancy watched him sink back in the big chair, almost out of sight, and she perched on a wooden chair in one corner and started to sketch the room. As she always did when designing, she forgot everything else and became totally involved with her own thoughts. She did one quick preliminary sketch after another, tossing out ideas and rendering them in broad strokes. Most of them would be discarded, but they would serve as a basis for triggering more ideas. She moved around the room and was conscious of Cassie standing in one of the two doorways to the big room, watching her. At one point she moved her chair out into the side hall to get a long-range shot through the doorway, sketching in an arched doorway instead of the square one that was there. When she stopped she saw Zachary standing by the stairway, almost as if he were standing guard by it. Finally, growing tired, she put down the sketch pad and decided to tour the rest of the ground floor of the house. Her throat had grown dry and she was thirsty. She went down the hallway to the kitchen that was to the right at the end, just past the dining room. Suddenly at the kitchen door she halted, frowning. How had she known where the kitchen was? She pushed open the door to look at the dark, gloomy old-fashioned kitchen with the huge iron stove and the open hearth with big black kettles hanging over it. It was there, just where she knew it would be. Had it been a lucky guess? No, she had to answer. She hadn't guessed, she'd known, as if she'd lived in the house. Perhaps, she told herself, it was a kind of subconscious logic, the result of poring over countless interior plans during three years at the academy. She found the tapwater cold and refreshing, and when she went back into the corridor, Cassie—just outside the door—startled her.

"I guess the kitchen could stand some redoing, too," Cassie said, her eyes dark, probing.

"It certainly could," Nancy said, returning to the living room. Cassie didn't follow her. She picked up her sketch pad and went upstairs. At the first-floor landing she paused to look up at the attic floor again, at the darkness of the winding stairway. When she turned to walk to her room she glimpsed Zachary crossing the corridor just at the foot of the steps. Had he been watching her, she wondered? She had the feeling he had, and so had Cassie. Nancy lay down on the bed and groaned, a deep groan that came from an inner anguish. No, she told herself, she wouldn't start thinking things like that again. Maybe they were watching her. They'd probably watch any newcomer to this strange, inwardly turned land out of plain old curiosity. The night was still in her body and her mind, she knew, and she fell into a half world of rest, a place not deep enough for dreams and not awake enough for thoughts. It was a world of her own she had learned to find in those times when dreams were something to fear. Finally she roused herself. It was nearly dinner time. She changed into a white dress with a V-neck, lightweight and sleeveless. The night promised to be muggy and humid, and the cicadas were already starting to chirp.

When she went downstairs, she found Samuel Howell had made bourbons and branch-water. She had one with him while dinner was being readied. There was a cook, she learned, a big-boned woman with brown stringy hair and a dull expression. But she could do wonders with ham, which was the main dish. Zachary, in a white bus-boy's jacket, served. Jodie came down in a skirt and white, scoop-necked blouse. Cassie stayed in her severe, high-necked, gray dress. Samuel Howell was garrulous, filled with anecdotes and questions smoothly woven in about her background. She found herself telling him things she hadn't thought of in years and years, things of her childhood, of her aunt and her uncle who had raised her.

"I remember once hearing the name Howell figured somewhere in my family tree," Nancy said. "But I don't suppose it would be any relation to your family here."

"No, no chance of that," Samuel Howell said, drawing on another bourbon. "The Howells here have never branched out. Folks here in Deepwell Valley, and in most of the Little Smokies, just don't go anywhere. We don't go outside and outsiders don't come here. Guess it's part of the nature of folks here. Why, you and that Pete Thatcher fellow are the only outsiders who've been here for I don't know how many years."

"But you must have some contacts with the outside world," Nancy said. "Delivery people, doctors, travelers."

"Only second hand, you might say," the huge man answered. "Anything we need is delivered to the railroad station, and folks go pick it up. Most folks do their own doctorin' up here. In emergencies we use Doc Sieboldt on the other side of the valley, and he's practically one of us. As for travelers, we don't get many. The roads here aren't even on any maps I ever seen."

"But you seem an educated man, Mr. Howell," Nancy said. "And Jodie and Cassie are not, well ... hillbillies."

"Pa's got outside interests, properties which pay rent, and he makes trips to them," Jodie said.

"And he had special teachers brought in for us kids, for Jodie and me," Cassie said. "When we were young, a teacher lived here with us for a long spell."

"So we're different from most folks here in the valley," Jodie said. "Pa runs Deepwell Valley, what there is to run."

Samuel Howell's deep laugh rumbled over the note of triumph and pride in Jodie's words. "Hush, now, Jodie, with that kind of talk," he said benignly, pleased to hear it. "Every place has some man or family that sort of leads it. I guess here it's the Howells. It always has been that way."

They were just starting on coffee when Nancy heard the door. Zachary hurried to answer it. The gaunt-faced man appeared a moment later and whispered to Samuel Howell. Nancy saw the big man's face darken and his bright eyes grow cold. Muttering apologies, Samuel Howell got up abruptly, moving quickly for all his bulk, and followed Zachary from the dining room. Cassie and Jodie carried on the conversation, Jodie talking about clothes, Cassie about her herb garden behind the right wing of the house. But Nancy could hear Samuel Howell's deep, rumbling voice from the living room—there was anger in it. Half phrases cut through to her. "You were told not to come till after midnight," she heard him say. The other man's murmured answer was lost but even his distant murmurings sounded a faint and frightened note. "No, not till later," she heard Howell say. "You'll have to wait." She didn't try to listen. Her ears just refused to obey her.

Finally Samuel Howell returned to finish coffee with her, his manner smooth, unctuous, without a trace of inner anger. Nancy wondered why he felt he had to bother for her sake. Or was it just an inbred preoccupation with outer appearances? But he did make an extra effort at appearing casual and calm. It would have been successful, had she not heard the anger in his voice only moments before. When they finished their coffee, Jodie stood up abruptly, almost stretching her lush, full body.

"I'm going out, Pa," she announced, and the voice of the Kentucky hills was in her tone again, flat, without a hint of speech refinement. Nancy saw Cassie's eyes follow her sister as Jodie strode from the table, hips swinging.

"I'm afraid I'm still very tired from my trip yesterday and that mix-up last night," Nancy said. "If you'll forgive me, I think I'll try to get to bed early."

"Why, sure," Samuel Howell said. "Nothin' like sleep to make a body feel better."

Samuel Howell walked her to the stairway and waited there until she reached the first-floor landing. Politeness, Nancy wondered as she waved goodnight, or was he, too, watching where she went. The corridor was unlighted and stretched before her—a long, black tunnel—to the closed door at the far end with the chairs wedged before it. She hurried to her room, turned on the lamp, and bolted the door behind her. After undressing, she turned down the bed, and put off the light. Opening the window, she let the few stray puffs of air cool her naked body. It was a hot, close night and the sweet smell of the thick foliage drifted into the room, the lush smell of trees and bushes and blooming shrubs of acacias, mountain lilacs, oaks and elms, sassafras, and sharbark. She ran her hands over her slender, lithe, lovely body and lay down across the bed in the dark and thought of Peter Thatcher. He had seen her this way, he and Dirk, and she was sorry for both, sorry she had not been awake for the one and sorry she had been for the other. Why did Dirk intrude so upon her today, she wondered. She had successfully kept him from creeping back into her thoughts, her conscious thoughts, anyway. She'd continue to do so, she told herself determinedly, knowing she had been told that this was the wrong way of handling it. But wrong or not, so far it had worked. And now, last night, all the old fears had been brought back again, fears of what was and what wasn't, fears of the nights that helped to blend the real into the unreal until there was no dividing line left.

She lay there and suddenly heard voices, Jodie's voice, first. She got up and went to the window, standing to the side and peering over the sill. Jodie and Cassie were below. There apparently was a side door beneath the window and Jodie had a light shawl in one hand.

"Who is it now, Jodie?" Nancy heard Cassie ask. "Where are you going?"

"None of your damned business," Jodie said, her voice cold steel.

"You'll tell me all about it later, won't you, Jodie?" Cassie asked, and Nancy was shocked by the abject, begging tone of her voice. The cold, sharp Cassie was pleading, almost whimpering. "Tomorrow, you can tell me about it tomorrow, Jodie," she said.

"And have you flap your big mouth off again?" Jodie answered cruelly.

"I won't, Jodie," Cassie pleaded. "I promise. I just want to hear a little bit."

"Maybe," Jodie said. "If you stay out of my things, hear?"

Cassie didn't answer and Nancy saw Jodie stride off. Cassie finally turned and Nancy heard the door softly open and close beneath her. She went back, put on a light, see-through peignoir and went to bed. She wondered what the little scene had meant but even without knowing, it somehow fitted this strange house and this strange land. Nothing was really quite what it seemed to be and Peter Thatcher was right about her being an "outlander." She had never been any place where she felt so completely apart from the inhabitants. Even the thick, lush green of the land seemed to be a kind of curtain. It was more than the feeling that comes with being a stranger. It was the awareness that one could never be anything but a stranger. She turned over and the weariness of her body drove her thoughts away finally. Sleep came, but it was a restless sleep that refused to close her mind from the terrifying scenes of the night before and she woke up twice, hands to her mouth, stifling a scream as she saw a wild-eyed creature with gaping mouth and sub-human face. But the girl lay down again each time and went back to sleep. She had grown used to such slumber. She had learned to fight the night for a few hours of sleep.

And so she was sleeping once again when the noise reached into her mind and she sat up, eyes snapping open. But there was only silence. She lay back down again and closed her eyes, listening. She lay there, waiting, and then she heard it again, a sliding, dragging sound—then the harsh sound of metal, of chains hitting against each other. It seemed to be outside, on the stairs and she lay very still, listening, hearing the sound of her own heart pounding. The sound had gone away, and then she heard it again, fainter now, the clank of chains again and then it faded away entirely. Nancy kept her eyes closed and felt her body slowly relax. She refused to wonder what it was, or what it wasn't. No, no, no! She heard her inner voice cry out. Not again. Don't wonder. Don't think about it. She drew a deep breath. She was here to do a job and that was all she'd let herself think about. She'd get on with it and leave here as quickly as possible. She had learned to fight the dark inner forces of the soul and she'd continue to do so.

Nancy had fought herself back to sleep when the scream woke her, a hoarse scream, a man's voice. She lay still and heard it again, distant, from outside, cries and strange sounds. She got up and ran to the window. The night mists had come up to cloak the land in thick, rolling grayness. But the moon was round and high and lighted the heavy, wispy patches that floated up from the hollows. The night fog lay on the ridge, and she saw someone running along the top of it, toward the line of trees that marched over the top at the far end. There was something else there, chasing the running figure. She strained her eyes to peer through the swirling mists that were caught by the moonlight. Was it an animal? She kept peering, and the running figure emerged in a moment's break in the mist. It was a man, unquestionably, and then the mist swirled back again, just as the pursuing shape started to appear. Nancy heard the sound again, this time a sharp, short cry, and then there was silence. She watched along the ridge, running her eyes back and forth over it, trying to pick out movement, shapes, forms where the moonlight speared the grayness. But the moonlight was a dancer shrouded in yards and yards of diaphanous veils that revealed nothing. She turned from the window and crawled back into the big bed. There had been something, though, a man running. She was sure of that. Nancy felt her teeth bite into her lower lip. She had been sure of last night, too. And she had been sure of so much in the past year. She buried her face into the pillow and went to sleep again.

Morning came sliding into the room on a shaft of sunlight, bright and pure and gold. The first thing Nancy did as she got up was to go to the window and peer out across the rolling hollows to the ridge. The ridge was bathed in sunlight—a warm inviting place—and there was no sign of anything unusual. Everything was, in fact, terribly soft and green, the hollows cool and softly shadowed. She heard a wood thrush sing, saw a lark take wing, followed by a red-winged blackbird. The hollows of darkness and nightbound mists, of eerie shadows and slipping shapes, were completely gone. This land wore two completely different faces, one by night and one by day, she realized again. But that was no more than fitting for a place of inward contradictions. Nancy dressed, putting on a loose skirt with deep pockets to carry her pencils and charcoal. She wanted to carry out some of yesterday's sketches more thoroughly. Unbolting the door made her feel slightly ashamed. The sunlight made everything so warm and bright and a world where bolts were totally unnecessary. But when she went outside she couldn't help glancing down at the dark end of the hall, at the closed door where the chairs were wedged. She frowned. One of the chairs seemed to be wedged sideways against the door, now. She would wager it hadn't been that way yesterday. Her lips tightened and she went downstairs, the brilliant sunlight unable to erase the memory of shuffling sounds and chains.

Cassie and Jodie were having breakfast in the dining room, griddle cakes and jam and toast and sausages. Nancy wanted only coffee.

"Pa's gone down to Deepwell for the morning," Jodie said in her flat, nasal delivery. "He'll be back later. If there's anything you want, just ask Cassie or me, hear now?"

Nancy smiled sweetly and nodded. Cassie was her usual angular, hard-edged self, Nancy saw, the older girl's eyes were shifting, darting, cold. She seemed the stronger, more commanding of the two girls, yet Nancy had learned differently last night. Jodie, in a tight shirt, opened low, and dungarees, was everything Cassie was not. There was an almost disturbing over-abundance to Jodie's succulence, something that went beyond mere sensual beauty. She was like a collection of tropical flowers Nancy recalled once seeing in a greenhouse, flowers so lush, so overpowering in their sensuality, as to seem almost obscene, an overripe kind of beauty. Nancy smiled inwardly. Anyone reading her thoughts would think it was pure envy. But Nancy knew better. She was happy enough with her own kind of beauty.

"I want to get a general idea of all the roooms this morning," Nancy said. "To see if I can find a general theme to develop for them all."

"All the rooms on the ground floor, of course," Cassie said, and Nancy wondered. Was that a warning again about wandering into forbidden areas of the house? Or was she just making too much of a simple statement. It didn't matter. She had more than enough to do and she had no wish to wander elsewhere in the huge house. She refused to think about her curiosity regarding the dark corridor and the semibarricaded door at the end. She finished her coffee and left Jodie and Cassie still at the table. With her big sketch pad, she wandered from the living room to the study and back again, then into the kitchen and the dining room and into a small room off the study that appeared to be an extra living room. It had possibilities for being turned into a smaller informal dining area. But there was no overall theme that lent itself to a cohesive treatment, and after numerous sketches she abandoned the idea. Each room would have to be redesigned on its own, with its own individual theme. She had worked hard all morning, and her back muscles were tight. She put down the sketch pad just as Samuel Howell entered the house. Nancy was in the small extra room when she saw him come in, Zachary behind him. He crossed the hallway on his way to the east wing of the house. The white linen suit was wet with perspiration, and she saw smudges of brown dirt on the sleeves. Nancy heard him going up the other stairway and then the sound of water being run.

She left her sketch pad by the door and went outside into the bright sun. It fell upon her and immediately sent its warm fingers into her tensed, stiff back. She walked slowly up the gentle incline on the soft thick grassy slope that led to the ridge. She crossed over to where the edge of the woods followed up the slope also and she noticed a small path emerging from the thick bushes. It was noticeable only when she passed almost directly in front of it, emerging alongside a thick oak tree with a huge, low branch that jutted out from the front of it. She'd noticed the tree from her window but hadn't seen the path. The ridge was higher up than it seemed, and when she reached it she sank down on the ground to catch her breath. She was at the very spot where she'd seen the man running in the night, she realized, and her eyes searched the ground. But the grass was thick and fresh and dotted with black-eyed Susans and orange milkweed. There were no tracks to be found here. Nancy lay back on the ridge and enjoyed the hot sunlight pouring down on her body. But there had been someone running here last night, a man being pursued. Or had there? She lay her arm across her eyes and her breasts started to rise and fall rhythmically as the questions flew through her mind again, bitter angry thoughts that had no answers. Had the night mists played tricks on her? She rebelled against the thought. There had been someone. She had seen him. And yet there was always yesterday, always the past year, pushing itself forward, intruding on her. How long would it continue to cling, trying to twist things, turning certainties into uncertainties, making her into a tower of self-doubt? How long could it cling without pulling her backwards?

Nancy sat up, her eyes troubled, a frown creasing the smoothness of her forehead. She gazed into the dark green of the trees just at her right. Her frown deepened. Something small, dark, raglike, lay under a bush. She leaned over, reached under the bush, and pulled it out. It wasn't a rag. It was a small cap, one of those peaked, blue-and-white-striped caps worn by railroad engineers. There was no mildew on it and time hadn't stiffened the fabric. It couldn't have lain there for very long. Her eyes went back to the spot where she'd seen it. She looked up, past the bush, where the trees widened. There were dark marks on the ground, there by a patch of leaves. The girl got to her feet and went into the line of the trees, kneeling down by the patch of leaves. The marks were sticky pools of liquid, drawing mosquitoes and other insects, dark red liquid that was already turning brown. Nancy swallowed and got to her feet. It was blood, unquestionably. She followed the few spots to the edge of the trees at the ridge and then they disappeared. She realized she was still holding the small, peaked cap in her hand and shoved it into the deep pocket of her skirt. What did the bloodstains mean? And the little cap? Was there any connection between them? The figure running on the ridge in the mists leaped into her mind at once but she fought down the impulse to let her thoughts run wild. There'd be none of that, not now. It was too dangerous for her, much too dangerous.

Nancy walked away quickly, down the soft grass of the slope. She reached Bloodroots Manor but kept walking, on past the big house, through the sea of star-pointed cream white blossoms and onto the little dirt road that led from the front of the house. She walked quickly, frowning, wondering and knowing only that she had to talk to Peter Thatcher. Besides, he had promised to take her to the old station today. This was most definitely the time for it. She hurried, a mixture of anticipations welling up inside her.

The road was longer, a lot longer than she remembered it, coming up in his battered old car, and she had to reverse herself twice when she realized she had taken wrong turns. She passed two men and an old, wrinkled prune of a woman in a long gray dress and white hair pulled up in a bun. The men, both younger, wore trousers and suspenders and nothing else but their shapeless felt hats. She smiled at them as she passed but they only stared back. Further along the road she met two children, barefoot, too, and only in shorts, their eyes deep and wide, hair long, unkempt. As she finally drew within sight of Peter Thatcher's cabin, she saw three men go into the thick woods across the road from his place, the woods she had fled through the other night. Her steps quickened, and she saw the cabin door was open. She was almost there when the figure moved from the trees, startling her, the guitar over one shoulder.

"Hello, Jed," Nancy smiled as the figure swung in beside her. He nodded, giving her a swift, sideways glance from those eyes of lightest blue. The small, elfin smile again played along his finely molded lips. He wore only the open vest and trousers, and his blond hair came down in tight little curls along the back of his neck. Once again she saw that Jed Batterbee was really quite handsome in his strange, delicate way. He was Pan, in the woods, with a guitar instead of pipes. Jed gracefully stepped back as she reached the doorstep and she heard the sound of Peter's tape recorder and Jed's voice on it singing a mountain song. Peter turned as she appeared in the doorway and he snapped off the recorder.

"I'm sorry," Nancy said. "I didn't mean to interrupt your work."

"That's all right," he said, getting up. He was still as tall and warm-eyed as she remembered. "I was just replaying that tape before packing it away," he said, his easy smile making her feel at once less like an intruder. "I was wondering if you'd really come down today."

"Why?" she asked him and he shrugged, his eyes dancing.

"Perhaps I thought you'd want to leave well enough alone," he said.

"Unfinished business," she said. "Besides, I owe you another thanks for the way you handled things yesterday when we got to Bloodroots. That was very understanding of you."

"But you still want to see the old station," he said evenly. She nodded quickly. I must, she added silently. I have to see it. I have to.

Peter Thatcher's hazel eyes watched her, thoughts just behind their orbs, but finally he only smiled. "The chariot awaits you," he said.

Jed Batterbee was standing just outside the door, and Nancy saw his eyes following them, staying on her. Peter gestured to the back seat of the battered old Ford and Jed lightly leaped in, his eyes narrowing in a kind of triumph. Peter drove the car down the road, deeper into the hollow, turning in a long circle that carried them along the thick woods that bordered the road. The deepest hollows inside the main hollow were wonderfully cool under a blanket of branches and the sun burst down on them with seemingly renewed force everytime they came up on flat land.

> " I know where I'm going,
>     And I know who's going with me,
> I know who I lo-ove,
>     But my dear knows who I'll marry...."

Jed's clear, light voice came from the back seat and Peter smiled. Nancy had the distinct feeling they were sharing a small private joke at her expense, but it was without malice, and she felt warm and contented here with Peter and this strange, fey boy. They passed a spire of smoke coming up from what seemed the very thickest part of the woods to their right.

"People are living in there?" Nancy asked in amazement.

"All over in there," Peter said. "That's Wolf Hollow, all of that woodland. The Ordways live there. It's strictly off-limits for anyone else."

"Even for the Howells?" she probed. "According to Jodie Howell, her Daddy runs Deepwell Valley if not all of the Little Smokies."

"That's pretty much true," Peter said. "Samuel Howell and the Ordways seem to have some sort of arrangement, as far as I can figure out. They're almost like gamekeepers for him. Maybe wards of a medieval lord would be more accurate."

"This place doesn't seem like it's in the twentieth century," Nancy commented.

"It isn't, really. And neither are the people." Peter turned a sharp curve and Nancy felt the small peaked cap in the pocket of her skirt.

"There's another reason I came to see you, Peter," she said. "Did you hear of anyone being killed last night? Or badly hurt?"

Peter frowned. "I haven't, but then I've been at the cabin all day," he said. He turned to Jed. "Hear anything like that Jed."

"Folks getting killed?" Jed said. "No, no, and I'd have heard if there'd been feuding and fighting."

It was the first thing Nancy had heard Jed say that wasn't sung and even this was spoken in a strange rolling way, more cadenced than spoken. "I was beginning to think you never talked, Jed," she smiled back at the blond figure. His eyes held hers levelly, their message undecipherable.

"I don't hardly," he said. "Singin's much better." The statement was delivered with a finality that closed the subject at once. "Care to elaborate on that question, Nancy?" Peter asked, and Nancy felt herself swallow. But Peter Thatcher's eyes were serious, unsmiling and level. There was a definite strength to this tall, rangy, mild-mannered man that warmed her. But still she swallowed hard.

"I want to tell you," she began. "But I don't want to be laughed at."

"I won't laugh," he said. "I won't believe, either, if I don't feel I can."

Nancy knew she couldn't ask for more and she told of waking in the night and the cries from the ridge. She didn't tell of the sounds of shuffling and chains but spoke only of what she'd seen on the ridge through the night mists. When she'd finished, Peter Thatcher shook his head but his hazel eyes as he looked at her, were kind, almost amused.

"You must be a damn good designer," he said. "You have a truly creative imagination."

Nancy felt her temper rise but he went on quickly. "First, the night mists play strange tricks on the eyes," he said. "I know that myself. You don't really know if you saw anything at all. Be honest, Nancy Hazleton."

The last stern admonishment was one Aunt Edna used to use and Nancy felt herself laugh. Then she grew serious again.

"Yes, I do know," she said. "I did see a figure running. I got a good look at it."

"It could have been an animal," Peter said.

"And the blood I found?" she flung out.

"From the same animal, probably being chased by another. The Little Smokies are filled with wild game, Nancy, and that includes bear."

"And this?" Nancy shot back, pulling out the little peaked railroad engineer's cap. "This was there under the brush."

Peter looked at the cap, holding it with one hand as he drove. "It could have belonged to anyone?" he said, his voice quiet, gentle.

"A railroad engineer's cap?" Nancy blurted back.

"They can be picked up almost anywhere, Nancy," Peter said. "All sorts of hats find their way into Deepwell Valley. One of the Ordway boys has a top hat. I've seen it myself. Tom Bounder has a yachtsman's hat, probably fell from a passing train. And Jed, here, has a good straw Panama he picked up someplace or other."

Nancy sat quietly, her fists clenched. She felt Peter's hand on her shoulder, his touch strong yet gentle, reassuring. It felt good. It was a long time since a man had touched her shoulder like that. "You're reaching too hard, Nancy," he said. "Since that first night you got here your mind has been primed to find wild, strange things. Give it a rest. Turn off that wonderful imagination of yours."

Nancy said nothing. There had been a man running on the ridge, she said silently. And that wonderful imagination had proven itself horribly, terrifyingly right all too recently to forget. But she said nothing and as the car took a little dip she looked up to see it rolling to a stop before the cobwebbed, boarded-up, deserted old station. It was the same one, she cried silently, the very same. She vaulted from the car and ran to it. Peter's long legs caught up to her as she stood on the rotted platform where the conductor had let her off. Her eyes went up to the top of the waiting-room roof where the big sign had been. There was nothing, only the oblong rectangle of wood where once a sign had obviously hung. The small sign on the cracked corner post wasn't there, either. There was nothing anywhere to label the station as Deepwell Junction. Only the boarded up windows, the dust and cobwebs and cracked wood were still the same. She was conscious of Peter standing silently beside her. She turned to look up at him, angry at the tears that welled up in her eyes.

"But they were there, Peter," she said. "They *were!*" Conscious of how weak her voice sounded, she walked to the edge of the platform and down to the road, her eyes frantically sweeping across the trees at the far side. But there was no sign there, either. She turned and started to walk as she had that night, up the road, and she felt Peter following along a few paces behind her. She walked and walked until she came to the small pathway that opened through the trees. The sign *Cottonwood Road* had hung there at the edge of it. But she saw through eyes misted over with tears, there was no sign, only the dark bark of the elm tree. She turned into the little passage, as she remembered doing the other night, when Peter's hand caught her arm.

"Not in there," he said. "That's part of Wolf Hollow. I'm not letting you get shot."

She let him pull her back onto the road. "Trespassing in Wolf Hollow is inviting a bullet. You came through part of it the other night because of the storm. Come on, Nancy. You've really seen enough, haven't you?"

She nodded, not daring to look up, ashamed of the tears staining her cheeks. It was no use to go further. There'd be no signs anywhere else, either, she knew. Peter held her arm as she walked down the road, head down. He halted before they neared the old station where Jed waited in the Ford. He lifted her face up and gazed into her eyes. She didn't even try to wipe the tears away.

"Come on, now, Nancy," he said softly. "There's no need to get so upset about it?"

"Isn't there?" she shot out angrily. He pulled her head down onto his chest and she clung to him. His hand on her back felt warm, strong, stilling the trembling in her body.

"Is there?" he asked quietly and she raised her head, her eyes answering him. "You've learned to cry without a sound, haven't you?" he said, a statement more than a question.

"Practice," she sniffed.

"Maybe you'll tell me about those reasons sometime?"

"Maybe."

"Till then, we'll both go with my guess about your panicking in the storm and stumbling into the old station," Peter said but she saw his lips tighten as he lifted her head again to look into her eyes. "You're stubborn, too, I see," he said. "You're a funny girl, Nancy Hazleton. You get to one."

She pressed against him. God, he certainly had gotten to her, she murmured silently. She didn't want to move out of the strong secure circle of his arms. But he turned and she walked back to the station with him. "You go on to the car," Peter said, waving at Jed. "I'll be right along."

Nancy pressed a handkerchief to her eyes and walked to the old car, climbing in, trying to smile brightly at Jed. She saw his light blue eyes search her face. His fingers strummed the guitar, his eyes danced as he sang.

*"I am a poor wayfarin' stranger,*
*A wanderin' through this world of woe."*

Nancy gazed at him, wondering if he mocked her, and yet she couldn't find mockery in his almost skyward glance. She found a smile for him.

She turned to see Peter squatted down beside the rusted tracks. He was running his hand over a section of them, looking at his fingers as he did so. When he came back to the car, his face was expressionless but there was a darkness in his eyes and he looked deeply into her own pupils, almost as though he were trying to find his way behind her outer self. His face suddenly creased in a slow grin and he patted her arm as he eased himself into the seat beside her. The engine coughed its way to life and they drove back along the road. Nancy had composed herself enough to try a whole sentence.

"I'm sorry I brought you all the way down here for nothing," she said.

"It wasn't for nothing," he said and she wondered at the hard grimness in his voice. But his tone changed instantly. "No time spent with you can be counted as wasted."

"Thanks," she said. "But I won't talk about it again. It was good of you to bring me here."

"Not that you're really convinced about anything," Peter Thatcher commented wryly, and Nancy felt the tears just back of her eyes again.

"I'm not convinced about anything, I guess," she said. "I'm not sure what I see or what I think or even what I know sometimes. I think we should just leave it at that."

"All right," Peter said. "If we can."

Nancy didn't look up at the implication of his words but they weren't lost on her. She knew she couldn't leave it at that inside herself. But she'd damn well try for now, anyway. Maybe time would unravel things by itself. It was always a hope. One that seldom worked out, though. She knew Peter cast anxious glances at her watching her struggle with herself and she made herself sit back and toss him a smile. She looked out at the lush, thick foliage and let a pheasant that waited by the roadside carry her mind to other things. As they rounded a curve Peter slowed the car abruptly and she saw the figures ahead, facing each other on both sides of the road. There were three men on one side and two men and two boys on the other. One of the boys and one man carried a rifle on one side, the two men on the other also held long-barreled rifles. The men wore trousers, torn cotton shirts and high-crowned felt hats. Everyone was shoeless. As Peter stopped the car she heard Jed land lightly on the road and saw him saunter past toward the figures.

"What is it, Peter? Nancy asked.

"The Ordways and the Gormans," Peter explained. "They're feuding clans. Jed will handle it. He usually does, anyway. It takes someone they both accept as neutral."

"The Ordways," Nancy echoed. "Aren't they the ones you said ruled Wolf Hollow?"

"Yes, but they're also part of a six-generation feud with the Gormans."

"About what?"

"I don't know that," Peter said. "I doubt most of the Ordways or Gormans know it, either. There might be an old patriarch or two that still remembers the origins, but the continued shootings and killings are enough for the others to keep the feud going."

Nancy watched Jed cross back and forth from side to side.

"They don't talk to each other," Peter said. "They just shoot at each other. That's why someone like Jed appearing at an accidental confrontation such as this seems to be can turn aside a shooting match."

"That means they really don't want to keep on feuding."

"No, it only means they want to fight when they've gotten ready for it. I've decided that there's a ritual and an element of the old religious wars in these feuds. A certain amount of killing and fighting is necessary to keep the faith, to give evidence of belief in their righteousness. But like the old religions, they recognize they have to exist together. The intermingling of those positions creates a kind of delicately balanced working arrangement."

"It's ridiculous and barbaric."

"Undoubtedly. But it probably keeps them from stagnating altogether in their own genetic mismatches."

"I didn't think things like this existed any longer."

"They do. They exist not only here in the Little Smokies but in all insular regions, in the family vendettas of the Sicilians, in the constant tribal wars of primitive regions, in the blood enmity of Arab tribes. It exists in many places and it's all part of the same syndrome, the huge interrelated family with its different branches in conflict. Generations of close breeding make the roots run deeper until they reach depths ordinary fights between ordinary people and groups never reach."

"It's terrifying," Nancy said. "No wonder the Howells call the manor Bloodroots. It's not only appropriate to the flower but to this entire valley. The ground is soaked with roots of blood."

Peter paused a moment, reflecting. "I never thought of it in that light but it certainly does fit," he said. He put a hand on her shoulder. "We've got to talk some more, Nancy Hazleton," he added. "A lot more."

"Yes, I think I'd like that," she said.

"Meanwhile, for the time being, suppose you agree to stop any nighttime excursions, for any reason. The night here can play strange tricks on a person. It has a way of getting to you."

"Agreed," Nancy said lightly. She moved away as Jed turned and started back to the car. She saw the Ordways move back into the deep, heavy woods and the Gormans walk on down the road. When Jed got into the car Peter drove on, not asking a thing of him. Nancy was bursting to inquire but she held her tongue. Asking right out was obviously not something done around here. They drove to the cabin in silence, and she had just climbed from the car and come around to the front of the cabin when Jodie appeared, coming down a small path just off to the right and behind the cabin.

"Well, Miss Nancy, you do get around," she said and there was little warmth in the smile she flashed. But her black brown eyes, big and round and liquid as a young deer's, made Nancy's heart flip and she heard the name *Dirk* flash in her mind. Dammit, she swore inwardly. She should be able to look at a pair of intense, deep eyes without thinking of Dirk. She was glad when Jodie Howell turned to Peter, taking his arm. When she noted that Peter didn't even look uncomfortable as she did, she felt something more than resentment flaring up inside her.

"You and I were going to have a barbecue out back, remember?" Jodie was saying to Peter. He nodded, sandy hair falling down over one eye.

"Of course I remember," he said. "I've got the chicken all cut and quartered, ready and waiting. I'll get a fire started."

He turned to Nancy then and his eyes were bland. "Thanks for stopping by with my things," he said. Nancy swallowed and nodded. His things were still in her room. She'd hurry back and put them at the bottom of her suitcase until she got a chance to bring them to him. Once more Peter had smoothed out an awkward place for her, realizing she wouldn't want the Howells to know why she had come down to see him. Once more she owed him a vote of thanks. She would have shown her appreciation if Jodie weren't hanging on his arm. She turned away and started up the road, feeling more angry than she had any right to feel.

# CHAPTER FOUR

S HE WAS HALF UP THE LITTLE INCLINE, consumed in her own resentments, before she realized Jed was silently padding along beside her. The little smile edged his lips and he held the guitar loosely in one hand. She smiled at him, grateful for his company and sorry she'd been so preoccupied. At the bend in the road she halted and looked back, as if she were looking at the view, but her eyes traveled straight down to the little cabin. Jodie stood close to Peter, hanging onto his arm, her big, full breasts pressing into his chest. And he didn't seem to mind one bit.

She felt the anger setting her jaw in a tight line and she was angry at herself. She had no right to feel this way. It was plain, old jealousy, and not just of Jodie the female, the voluptuous, sensuous package that she was. She felt jealous of Jodie the person and what she could offer Peter beyond herself. She could undoubtedly help him with his work and was probably making the most of that, too. Was it Peter she had gone out to see last night, Nancy wondered, and grew angrier by the second. How much of herself had Jodie already given to Peter? And how much had he accepted? She flung the questions from her angrily, turned and strode on. She had almost forgotten about Jed again until she heard the sound of the guitar chord and his light, clear, sweet voice.

*"Hi, said the bluebird as she flew,*
*If I were a young man I'd have two,*
*If one got saucy and wanted to go,*

*I'd have a new string for my bow,*
*How-de-dowdy, diddle-o-day....*"

Nancy stopped and found herself glaring at Jed Batterbee. His smile was enigmatic, unperturbed.

"Was that supposed to be funny?" Nancy snapped, and then suddenly found herself laughing as Jed never changed expression but regarded her with a secret wisdom not so secret now. "I guess I deserved that," she said, linking her arm into Jed's. "Come on, walk me on a little further." Jed's smile deepened and his eyes traveled over her with a strange, almost distant sort of appreciation, as though he were admiring a flower. She walked briskly. The hills were always steeper than they appeared. They were nearing the big manor house when Nancy saw a green spot that was cleared in from the little road. She went over to it and lay down on the grass, welcoming the rest. Jed sat close to her, and his light, light blue eyes again caressed her body. It gave her a strange feeling for his eyes seemed to be able to see right through her clothes. She watched them travel along the line of her shoulders, then down to her breasts, circle there, linger, tracing the soft firmness of her there, and then move down to her flat stomach, down to the swell of her abdomen, and the converging lines of her thighs. Yet there was no animal desire in his gaze. Instead there was a tenderness in his eyes, a wistful sort of expression, almost a spiritual kind of longing. He was indeed something unique, this strange person, this throwback to Pan and his pipes. How really simple was he, Nancy wondered. Or how dangerous? The simple were very often the most dangerous, unchecked by normal inhibitions. And yet she could feel no fear in his presence. She sat up and looked at him, her eyes holding his. His gaze didn't waver, the sly little smile didn't change.

"What makes you go around being the troubadour of the valley, Jed?" Nancy asked. "What are you really like?"

He struck a chord and his eyes grew just the smallest bit softer as he sang to her.

*"Hi, said the little leather-winged bat,*
   *I'll tell you the reason that,*
*The reason that I fly through the night,*
   *Is because the Lord's my heart's delight.*
*Howdy-dow-dee diddle-o-day, howdy-dow-dee,*
   *Diddle-o-day...."*

"Have you a girl of your own, Jed?" Nancy questioned. "Or have you ever had one?" The smile slipped away so suddenly Nancy was almost shocked by it. He sang, a deeper quality in his voice.

*"Eyes like the morning star,*
   *Cheeks like the rose,*
*Laura was a pretty girl, God almighty knows,*
   *Weep, all ye little rains,*
*Wail, winds, wail,*
   *All along along the Colorado Trail...."*

"What do you think of Miss Jodie?" Nancy asked. Jed got to his feet with a light, elfin spring, his smile wider now. He strummed a chord with his fingers, bowed, and walked away, half-skipping, half-striding. Nancy watched for a moment and then rose to go herself. He had told her things, things that would take more deciphering, more pulling apart to find the meaning wrapped inside them. But she knew she'd found a friend in the strange, shy Jed Batterbee, a friend who was taken with her. That much was clear from his songs with their oblique statements lurking behind the words. It was strange, Nancy paused to wonder, why she should feel the need of a friend here in Deepwell Valley in the Little Smokies. Yet she obviously did feel that way.

She hurried on, the big white house beyond the fields of white flowers taking on a blue tint as the sun lowered. The sight of the sinking sun made her grow tense and she was furious with herself. The time when she dreaded the night was supposed to be over. Yet here she was, doing it again.

Samuel Howell on the porch of the house greeted her as she came in. "Been waiting to have my branch water and bourbon with you, Miss Nancy," he said.

"Very nice of you," Nancy said. "I took back the clothes that Peter Thatcher lent me the other night."

She followed Samuel Howell inside and eagerly took the bourbon he gave her. It was strong, comforting as it curled inside her. Cassie came into the living room but didn't take a drink. Nancy had a second as she thought of Jodie at her barbecue with Peter. "I met Jodie," Nancy said, suddenly feeling malicious, watching Cassie out of the corner of her eye. "She won't be here for dinner in case she hasn't told you. She and Peter Thatcher are having a barbecue at his place."

She was ashamed at the satisfaction she felt as she saw Cassie's lips tighten and the line of her jaw grow taut. Of course, Nancy realized, it was only a case of misery wanting company. But she was surprised at how Samuel Howell's huge face seemed to settle itself with a cheshire cat expression.

"That's right nice for Jodie," he said simply, but Nancy couldn't help feeling that there was something more behind that simple statement. Zachary appeared noiselessly to announce that dinner was ready and this time, at the table, Nancy didn't refuse to join Samuel Howell in another bourbon. Under the table, her leg pressed up against the wooden edge, and the small peaked cap in her skirt pocket suddenly made itself felt. With it, the night and the events of the day rushed back at her, and she was suddenly glad dinner was proceeding without a lot of small talk. She wanted to be alone. The darkness was already wrapping itself around the big house and the girl didn't trust her own powers of pretending. As soon as the meal ended, she took her sketch pad from the spot where she'd left it.

"If you don't mind, I'm going to my room and rework some of the ideas I tried out today," Nancy said. No one objected and she hurried upstairs into the darkness of the long corridor, her eyes traveling to the end of it again. She closed and bolted the door of her room, turned on the small lamp, and tried to rework her sketches. She managed a few and then put the pad down. She took off her clothes, taking the little cap from the pocket angrily, wanting to throw it away. But not out the window where it'd be found and perhaps questions asked. She stuffed it into the topmost corner of the shelf of the closet where it would be out of sight, unable to remind her of things that needed no reminding. But, turning out the light and sinking down on the bed, she knew the little cap had already done its work. It had opened the floodgates, and thoughts rushed over her with frightening persistence, like waves crashing over a rock, demanding recognition each time. She knew the feeling well, and suddenly she was standing at the deserted old station again with Peter beside her, looking vainly for the signs that weren't there. The terrible, bottomless void that had once opened up inside her opened up again now, a whirlpool sucking her under helplessly. She had so wanted those signs to be there. She couldn't blame Peter for what he thought. The same thoughts were hers. If there were no signs, then was there ever a primordial creature of terror? But whereas to Peter it was just a simple case of frightened imagination, to Nancy it was a horror more real than facing that creature again. Her body trembled and grew cold despite the hot, cloying thickness of the night. Real and unreal, Nancy murmured to herself. Fact and fancy. She couldn't fight that battle again. She might not win, this time. That was the most frightening of all the fears that leaped out at her from the past. That and the fact that the victory she thought she'd won, she had perhaps not won at all. So there had to have been signs, despite what she had seen with her own eyes this afternoon, and there had to have been that demoniac creature. It all had to have happened, not because logic dictated it. Logic said the very opposite. But sanity dictated it, that thin grip on sanity she would not give up.

Nancy rose and slipped on a robe. She'd hoped the bourbons would have helped her to go to sleep but she was wide awake. She got up, slipped on a robe, and unlocked the door. She'd get a glass of hot milk in the kitchen. That usually helped. The hallway was dark but there was still a light on downstairs and it reflected up the stairway, outlining the cherry bannister. Nancy hurried downstairs and into the kitchen where she found milk, fresh honey, and a small iron pot to heat it in. She had just finished and cleaned the glass when she heard the front door open and close. She stepped to the kitchen door to see Jodie come into the foyer. The girl's black brown soft eyes glanced up the staircase for a moment, her chin lifted arrogantly, and Nancy again groaned inwardly as memory stabbed at her. It was strange, she mused, helpless to stop herself, how her world had shattered after she'd met Dirk. Was he fated to keep on shattering her world, she wondered. She watched Jodie move on, out of sight, and waited till she heard the girl's footsteps on the other stairway before hurrying back to her room. Upstairs, the long, black hallway sent a chill down her spine, and she was glad to get inside the room and lock the door at once. She undressed quickly and went to bed but sleep still lingered before coming to her. Finally, her eyes closed against the dark.

She didn't know how many hours had passed when she woke and felt the coldness of her body. She lay very still in the bed, listening for whatever had wakened her and then she heard it, the shuffling noise again and the faint clank of metal, of chains. It seemed to come from outside the door, and then she heard the top step of the stairway creak. The sound of the chains came through again, and Nancy didn't move until the house was still and silent once more. Then she got up and went to the window.

Once again the night mists covered the hills and hollows, coating the ridge with a gray line. Yet there was someone out there. She could feel it and her eyes caught the dark bulk of a figure. Or perhaps it was only an animal. A puff of wind blew a hole in the thick mist and she saw what seemed a figure standing partially up the slope leading to the ridge. Nancy felt her impatience flare. The mists rose up from the ground to lay in mid-air, swirling and obscuring her vision as she looked down from the window. But out there, on the ground, she'd be able to peer under the trailing vapors. She went to the closet, put slacks and a sweater on over her nakedness and, unbolting the door, hurried out into the hall. The light from downstairs was out, and the house was pitch black. She felt her way along the wall to the stairway. Downstairs, she moved along the hallway, past the living room, past the kitchen. The side door beneath her window would be along the west wall. She felt for a few steps down to a dropped level that led to the basement and to the side door and once again she stopped. How did she know the side door would be by the basement steps? A logical guess again? No, Nancy breathed softly. She knew it, just as she had known where the kitchen was here in this house. Still frowning, she found the door and opened it to stand out on the grass by the side of the house.

At least she'd been right about the mist. She could see much more clearly beneath its heavier layers that rose upwards. She moved forward, walking through the swirling mist, peering ahead, pausing to listen and then walking on again. Finally she turned back. There had been no sounds, no figures in the night. Only the soft, clutching vaporous mists had floated before her eyes. She hurried back to the house, going into the side door again, finding her way back upstairs in the inky blackness of the halls. In her room she buried her face into the pillow.

"Oh please, God, no more nightmares," she whispered aloud. "No more hearing and seeing what isn't there. Please, please, please. Hasn't there been enough?"

Nancy sobbed silently and finally went to sleep, her pillow wet with tears. She slept soundly, now, with the fatigue of nervous exhaustion, and morning found her surprisingly refreshed. She put on slacks and a light blouse, tailored, of cream white nylon. The house was silent when she went downstairs. Only Cassie was about in the kitchen and the older girl was even more abrupt than usual. Nancy took coffee and started to work with her sketch pad at once. She was working up some definite ideas for the living room and the dining room, pleased with the way her drawings were taking shape. She was only partially aware of the desire to leave Bloodroots that sped her mind and pencil. During the night, her subconscious mind had concluded that this strange land wasn't the place for her, not now, not yet. The past was still too near, she had learned here, and she was still too easily thrown back to it. But she had contracted to do the job, and it would be a wonderful feather in her professional cap when she returned to the city to seek more work. She paused to wonder how the Howells would go about getting the fabrics and materials her new designs would demand. The painting and carpentry work would no doubt fall to Zachary. The man passed the doorway just as her thoughts had turned to him, and she answered his dour glance with a warm smile. The morning had grown very hot and suddenly she realized that most of it was gone. She put down the pad and went outside into the brightness of the day.

Jodie was walking down the slope from the ridge, her full, lush figure exuding an animal magnetism even in the shapeless, loose robe she had on. She was drying her wet hair with a towel.

"You like to swim, Miss Nancy?" Jodie asked and Nancy nodded. "Well, then you ought to get yourself up to Rock Lake," the girl went on. "Over the ridge and up the steep trail between the twin birches. It's a man-made lake in the middle of a rocky place, but it's quiet and away from everything. You can swim there in nothin' at all, which is what I was just doing. It's great, 'specially on a hot day like this."

Jodie went on and Nancy watched her go into the house. The idea of a cool swim in fresh, clear water appealed to her. And the few times she had gone swimming in the nude had been a wonderfully free, exhilarating sensation. She found herself walking up toward the ridge, ignoring the trees at the right where she'd found the blood and the little cap. She crossed over the ridge, saw the twin birches and the small trail between them, and followed it. The path led upwards sharply, and she grabbed at branches to pull herself along. It ended abruptly, and she found herself gazing at a small lake set into a hollow surrounded by rocks. The water was crystal clear and sparkled in the sun. Looking across at the far end, the small waterfall came down the rocks, and following the line of it upwards she saw the two wooden sluice gates atop the rocks. The little lake, really a giant pond, had been formed by diverting water from what was obviously a big lake back of the rocks above. The water sparkled at her, beckoning. Nancy glanced about. She was alone. She whipped off her clothes, feeling daring, and plunged into the little lake. The water was exhilaratingly cool on her hot skin, and she swam leisurely back and forth across the crystal-clear pond. She floated, letting the warmth of the sun and the cool of the water combine to work into her body, soothing, relaxing, invigorating. She felt completely free, a wood nymph luxuriating in her own private kingdom of nature, and indeed her long, slender body fit the role perfectly. The sun glistened on the drops of water on her skin and her beauty almost gleamed. She had reached the center of the little lake, swimming lazily, twisting and turning in the water, when a sudden roaring split the air, almost the sound of an explosion but not as sharp.

Nancy glanced up and saw the wall of water cascading down the rocks from the sluice gates, now wide open. It was already slamming down into the far side of the little lake, striking with the force of a runaway locomotive. The water of the lake was already rising angrily, starting to lift her body with it. In moments the entire little pond would be a seething cauldron of raging water as the torrent continued to hurtle down from the open sluice gates. She would be caught up in a maelstrom of fury, slammed against the rocks, and killed. The girl struck out for the shore, knowing she could never reach it in time. But the urge for survival knew no other course. The water was lifting her now, boiling up under the surface as the force of the roaring cascade drove it upwards and outwards. She felt herself torn around, sent skittering upwards as though a giant hand were holding her up. Nancy fought to get control but it was impossible. Now surface waves slammed into her, rolling cascades of water, turning her naked form over like a matchstick. She gasped as a mouthful of water crashed into her. She was rolling helplessly, trying to keep from drowning, a lovely center of a whirling, bubbling, frothing mass of water. She got a moment to see the rocks just ahead, the new water raising the level of the little lake instantly.

There was a shouting in her ears, dim first, then louder, mingling with the roar of the waterfall. She heard her name and fought back against the force of the water, feeling like a salmon fighting its way upstream. She glimpsed the tall, sandy-haired figure on top of the rock, a rope in his hand.

"Nancy, grab the rope," she heard him shout. Her head bobbed up as she kept pumping her arms and legs, fighting the water. The rope sailed out and struck her. She managed to get a hand on it, then two hands. She felt herself being pulled, her body swinging free, slamming against a rock, the pain nearly making her let go. But she clung and the rope was pulling her, dragging her sideways and forward through the water. Another rock scraped against her, and now she was along the rocks of the sides, themselves almost covered with the rapidly rising water. But now she felt strong hands pulling her arms, lifting her up onto the top of the flat rock. She was too terrified, too exhausted to think about her nakedness. Besides, with a sudden flash of grim humor, this was getting to be a habit with Peter Thatcher. She felt him lift her. "Quick," he said. "The water will be over the top of the rocks in a minute." He had her hand and was pulling her down the incline from the rocks, running, running down the leafy wooded area. Finally he halted and she fell against him, her wet body trembling. His arms were around her and she felt him move and he was handing her his shirt. She slipped it on quickly. It was more than long enough to make her quite modest.

"Not that I didn't like the view, but we're apt to bump into Jed or someone else," Peter grinned at her.

Behind her, she heard the sound of the water cascading over the rocks, overflowing the little lake and start-down the mountain. She looked up at Peter, fright in her eyes.

"It'll go down the gulleys and run-offs," he said, reading her thoughts. "It'll soak the land around here for a bit, but that's all. Somebody will call the Sheriff's office in Deepwell, and they'll close the sluice gates again."

He led her through narrow trails that magically brought them to his cabin. She was glad for his strength, his knowledge of the land and as they emerged just back of the cabin and she saw Jed by the doorway, she pulled Peter back.

"I owe you my life again, Peter," she said. His body was lean, hard-muscled, and he drew her to him, his hand large enough to completely cover her face, but so very gentle.

"I just happened to be at the right spot at the right time," he said. "I often walk up along that trail, and I usually take a length of rope with me wherever I go in these hills."

She felt a rush of something more than gratitude for this tall, sandy-haired man, a feeling she had thought she'd perhaps never have again. His hazel eyes looked deeply into hers and then he turned and led her to the cabin. Jed's light blue orbs gazed at her with his usual indecipherable expression, though she wondered if she hadn't caught a glimpse of curiosity. He followed them into the cabin where Nancy dried her hair with a towel Peter gave her. She decided to forego his offer of another oversized pair of trousers. His shirt, on her, was no shorter than an average mini-skirt.

"Someone opened the sluice gates and Nancy was in Rock Lake," Peter told Ted.

"On purpose," Nancy said, surprising herself. She saw Peter's frown. But she had said it and the thought had exploded inside her.

"Yes, on purpose," Peter said. "But whoever did it probably never even looked to see if anyone was swimming in Rock Lake." Nancy said nothing and took the cup of tea he gave her. He came around to face her, frowning.

"Do you really think someone tried to kill you on purpose?" he asked.

"I don't know what to think," Nancy said. "But a lot of very funny things have happened to me since I came out here, from the very first night.

"That sub-human creature again?" Peter said, and this time there was a sharp edge of sarcasm to his voice. Nancy felt her temper erupt.

"Yes, that sub-human creature again," she said. "He was real, dammit, real. And from what I've seen of this place something sub-human is more than possible. It could be out there in the wilds, anything could hide and live in these thick forests. Maybe it saw me and had the vestigial intelligence to open the sluice gates."

"Nancy, Nancy," Peter admonished, sighing deeply. She glared at him. "The last time the sluice gates were opened it was the Gannon kids. They wanted to make the big waterfall go. The time before that it was old Zeb Arkle. He just felt the main lake was getting high and he wanted to drain it some."

Pete turned to Jed. "Ask Jed," he said to Nancy. "He'll bear out what I've said." She watched Jed nod his head gravely, and she glowered at both of them. Inside her there was a churning. Peter could be so patiently tolerant because nothing that had happened had really happened in his mind. She kept her lips compressed tightly and looked out the door.

"I thought after that business with the signs at the old station," Peter began, but Nancy cut him off angrily.

"You thought wrong," she snapped and saw him shrug.

"I guess so," he said. "I thought you weren't going to wander around in the night anymore, either."

Nancy tried to keep the surprise from her eyes and knew she'd failed. "What makes you say that?" she asked.

"You were out wandering in the fog last night," he said matter-of-factly. "Jed saw you," he said matter-of-factly.

"How do you know it was me?" she tried again. "It could have been anyone in the fog, Jodie, Cassie." She looked at Jed and Peter glanced at him. "Well, Jed?" he asked, but she had the impression he was merely asking to satisfy her and pin her down.

*"I know my love by her way of walkin'*
  *And I know my love by her way of talkin'*
*And I know my love by her suit of blue...."*

Nancy knew the song herself. It was derived from an old Irish folk tune. And she also knew the meaning of the words.

"All right," she admitted grudgingly. "I heard noises again last night. I decided to go out and see for myself."

She saw Jed's smile widen, and he got up and silently padded from the cabin. Nancy found Peter's eyes and he came closer to her, his hand reaching out and cupping her chin.

"What am I going to do about you?" he asked, and his eyes were dark with concern. "Or perhaps I should ask what are you going to do about yourself?"

"What makes you think I have to do anything about myself?" she flared up at him. "I tell you a lot of very weird things have been happening to me here. Why don't you try believing me for a change?"

She didn't hide the anger in her voice. It was there. She wanted so desperately to have him believe her.

"I'd like to," he said simply. "Maybe I could if I were sure you believed in yourself."

His words were a shaft, striking to the very inner core of her. The gentleness of his tone did little to dull the accuracy of his words, and she felt the tears immediately spring into her eyes. His arms were around her, pulling her to him, and his lips were on hers. She opened her mouth for him, clinging to the strong smoothness of his bare chest. His lips were saying another kind of message now and she was answering, almost weak with the wonderful warmth of the feeling that spread out inside her, reaching out to every part of her body.

"Are you just being kind?" she finally asked, pulling away but still keeping the warmth of his body against hers.

"I'm never just kind," he grinned down at her.

"Yes, you are, that's just the trouble," she answered. "But I'm glad for it anyway." She leaned into his arms again but his words still lodged inside her. How much did she believe in herself? That was it, really, all there in that one question. How much did she? How much could she?

The happy closeness in Peter's arms suddenly exploded as two shots rang out and shouts echoed from the road outside. Nancy jumped in fright and Peter pulled her down to the floor. Another shot echoed, farther up the road, and then more shouts and Peter stood up, pulling her up with him. Her breasts under the shirt had pressed into him as they'd huddled on the floor and his eyes danced as he looked down at her.

"We must do that again sometime," he said.

"I'll ignore you," Nancy answered. "What was that, the Ordways and the Gormans again?

"No, the Gannons and the Meekers this time," Peter said. "Jed told me he'd heard there was going to be shooting. One of the Meekers got into an argument at Pop Warman's store with Hawk Gannon over the unsettled water rights to the stream on the down side of Wolf Hollow. Three generations of Gannons and Meekers have been fighting over that stream."

"Don't they ever let go of the past?" Nancy said acidly.

"Do you?" Peter asked, his voice quiet. She turned to face him and her chin lifted defiantly.

"I'd let go of it," she said. "It won't let go of me." She held his gaze for a long moment and then looked away. She hadn't said it was the past that made it impossible for her to believe in herself. She didn't have to say it. She knew Peter understood. She felt his hand on her shoulder, pushing her down on the edge of the bed against the wall.

"You say believe in you for a change when you really mean help you believe in yourself," he said.

"Perhaps that is what I mean," Nancy said softly.

"Then you've got to tell me everything about that past that's not so very past," Peter said. "Without knowing, I can't believe you or help you believe yourself. I can't say right or wrong to you. I can't even help you in what not to believe. Without knowing everything, I can't even find a way to help."

Nancy looked into Peter's eyes and the unspoken things she saw there, and suddenly she knew she had to tell him everything, every last terrible part of it. She had to tell him for his sake. She had to tell him for herself. She had to tell him for the promise that tomorrow held, the promise she glimpsed in the way he looked at her, the promise that gathered eagerly inside herself. And she had to tell him because she felt herself slipping backwards, a thread unraveling. Maybe Peter could help stop that. Maybe he could replace her cold fears with a normal determined rational self. She had to try. She lay back on the bed and began to talk to Peter as he sat down on the wooden chair and listened. She thought of others who had sat and listened to her as she lay on a couch and spoke to them, doctors, therapists. But there was a difference, now. The others had had to probe, to pull things from her subconscious. But now she wanted to tell Peter everything, no matter how horribly painful it would be in the telling. It was the only way.

The pictures already began to fill her mind, real, crystal clear as she started to relive a part of her life she had hardly just finished.

# CHAPTER FIVE

"DIRK, MY DARLING," THE GIRL WAS SAYING, holding herself close to the slender young man. "Tomorrow morning, Dirk, tomorrow morning. It will come so fast for me."

"For me, too, my sweet," the man said. The girl looked up at his face, his eyes deep, unfathomable magnets, luminous pools that could sweep her up with a glance. She closed her eyes as he bent his head down and moved his lips across her face, tracing a line over her eyebrows, down the side of her soft cheek, along the line of her jaw, soft as butterfly's wings. Then he drew back, and she opened her eyes to watch him leave, his face so smooth, so handsome, with the fine lips and slightly arrogant lift to his chin of a Raphael drawing. She closed the door to her small apartment and still his delicate face stayed with her. Tomorrow she would be his, in his arms forever and ever. Tomorrow they were running away to Maryland to be married, three months to the day when he'd come up to her at the school and speared her with those deep, liquid eyes. She remembered every moment of that first meeting. The Academy of Interior Design was not like a college where seniors and freshmen hardly even talk. Everyone mixed there, and it made no difference that she only had six months to go and he had just enrolled. He was more than the handsomest man she'd ever seen. He was beautiful, every line, every plane, every angle of his face a thing of symmetry and beauty. She guessed she had fallen in love with him right then and there. And he with her because he had pursued her ardently and sweepingly every moment since then.

Dirk, Dirk, my beautiful, wonderful Dirk, the girl said to herself as she undressed. He was so different from any man she'd ever known. Not that she'd known that many. She had actually lived a fairly sheltered life before coming to the city to attend the Academy and get her own apartment. Raised by her Aunt and Uncle who, like most older childless couples, outdid natural parents in protectiveness, she had been carefully watched and sent only to specially supervised schools. She had been demanding in her own standards, too, and her contacts with boys had always left her with disappointment if not disdain. And always feeling somehow alone, despite the love of Aunt Edna and Uncle Max, she found Dirk unflawed, unparalleled. She recalled once, soon after they'd met, he'd asked her about her background and how refreshingly different his reactions had been.

"I can't tell you much about my family background," she had admitted honestly. "My mother and father were killed in an auto accident when I was five. A driverless truck ran down a hill into them while they were stopped for traffic. I would have been killed along with them but that very morning I'd popped up with a case of measles and had to be left home."

"And your aunt never told you anything more about your family?" Dirk had probed.

"No, Aunt Edna never liked to talk about tragic things," Nancy said. "I'm afraid I just don't know much about my family tree."

"That's good," Dirk said, almost to himself.

"Why is it good?" Nancy recalled frowning.

"Well, I mean, I think the less we knew about our backgrounds, the more we'd relate to each other as individuals without a lot of family history, old prejudices, and ingrained ideas."

Maybe it wasn't too logical, but it was wonderfully different and romantic and that's all that mattered. It was like Dirk's courtship, filled with little notes, small attentions, and unexpected surprises. It was all almost too wonderful to believe, one of those marvelous once-in-a-lifetime things that sometimes happen. She was an incurable romantic herself, and she had always wondered if she could ever meet a man who felt as she did. And now there was Dirk, certainly the perfect romantic himself. She even liked his somewhat arrogant way of looking down at her, making her feel very small and helpless. When he proposed running off to get married, she felt weak with happiness. She knew Aunt Edna and Uncle Max would oppose any idea of marriage to someone she'd only known for three months. But of course they couldn't know Dirk and what he was like, the singular way he had made her into the all-important thing in his world. And himself in hers. So she'd wanted to at least write them, Edna and Max, or perhaps call them. But Dirk had been adamant and made her see it was better not to say anything till they were married. "Afterwards, when it's our own *fait accompli*," he had said and she'd agreed, of course.

The morning came on wings of glory and they flew to Maryland to marry. She didn't even mind the hurried atmosphere, the paid witnesses, the genteel shabbiness of it all. Or at least she made herself not mind. She was married to Dirk and that made up for everything else. She was the luckiest girl in the world, she told herself. Naïve little Nancy they had called her in school and they had been right, of course. Her romanticism had always been a kind of protective cloak, keeping away reality as well as sordidness.

They took the night plane back to the city. It had been decided they'd live in her apartment, and Dirk insisted on leaving school and getting a job. He'd already secured one in a department store, in fact. The apartment was big enough for the two of them, on the tenth floor with windows facing the street and a nice view of the skyline. As Dirk opened the door of the apartment, Nancy pinched herself to make sure it wasn't a dream. But it wasn't. She was Mrs. Dirk Bender.

And so, on her wedding night, it began. While she began to prepare for bed, Dirk told her he was going for a walk. She smiled secretly. It was typical of him, considerate, giving her time to be alone, to prepare herself. She didn't have the boldness to tell him she wasn't the least bit apprehensive. He'd find that out soon enough. The bedroom without lights on was light enough to see from the moon and dark enough for everything else. It was summer and hot and she left the windows open. She put on a filmy nightgown, a see-through affair, and lay down on the bed. Dirk took a long time to return, over an hour, and when he came in, he undressed in the dark in the bathroom. He was naked when he came to bed, slender, strong, a body like a young sapling, smooth and beautiful as his face. She felt her own body tremble for him. She saw his deep black-brown eyes travel over her as he stood beside the bed. But they held no desire. Instead, it was an appraisal, a cool, appraising survey, as though he were comparing her to other women he'd known. Of course she had to expect that, she told herself, but she felt just a little hurt anyway. Finally he lay down beside her, drawing the sheet over him. "Good night, Nancy," he said.

Nancy lay still, her heart whirling, a terrible emptiness sweeping over her. "Dirk," she finally said. "You're disappointed in me, aren't you? My body disappoints you."

"Of course not," he said, turning toward her. "But we're going to do things my way. Trust me. It'll be that much more wonderful. Do you know how many marriages are ruined on the wedding night? It's all haste and hurry, everyone trying and no one really ready. A woman should be like a parched man at an oasis. Then it's an unforgettable experience, and things are started off right."

I'm parched, Dirk, she wanted to say. I'm ready. But she kept silent. He was so much wiser, so much more experienced in these matters than she. Of course she would trust him.

"When I make love to you it'll be something special," he said. "Now good night, darling." He turned on his side and was asleep in minutes. She lay awake, seeing his naked body come toward her, wanting him so much. She lay a hand on his hard, smooth body as he slept. Maybe it was better this way, his way, she told herself. He was there beside her and that was all that counted. The rest would come. She finally went to sleep.

That was the first night of the nightmare that grew and grew and held her under the spell of it. The next night Dirk wore pajamas to bed and he held her tenderly, almost brotherly, making sure not to do more than that. He had gone out for a long walk again before coming to bed. But she was content just to be in his arms. She loved him so that just being near him was happiness. Yet her body ached for his, despite herself. The nights that followed that week were the same. During the day she went to school and he to work. They usually dined out at a small restaurant and Dirk was his romantic, charming, solicitous self. She was so proud to be his as she saw other women turn to look at him as they walked by. But each night he took his walk. Some were longer than others. And each night she lay awake for his return. Sometimes he would come to bed naked, standing before her, looking down at her, and she wondered how he could be so completely unaroused by the sight of her. Then one night he caressed her with his hands and his lips until she thought she would explode. But then he just lay down beside her and went to sleep. She clung to his back that night, until her body ceased its trembling.

Then one night, they'd gone to a movie and it was late when they got back to the apartment. Dirk didn't take his usual walk. Nancy waited in bed while he was in the bathroom. This time she didn't put on even the filmy nightgown but let her lovely, slender body spread naked across the bed. When he came in he stopped short, and she thought she saw a strange panic leap into his deep eyes. "What do you think you're doing?" he said, a harshness in his voice.

"Seducing you," she said and was surprised to hear the sharp bitterness of her own voice. "Seducing my husband." He was at the edge of the bed, wearing only the bottom of his pajamas. She sat up and flung herself on him. "God, Dirk, make love to me," she said desperately. "I'm on fire." He tried to push her aside but she clung to him, pulling him down on top of her, and for the first time she felt his body respond to her. He pressed upon her, his hands moving up and down her skin, making her quiver from head to toe. He was trembling, too, now, and she heard his breathing harsh, almost angry. He was going to make love to her. She reached down, all her inhibitions drowned by the nights of frustrated waiting. And then, with a roar, he tore from her, sweeping her from the bed with his arm. She fell to the floor, crying out. But the pain was inside, not outside. She glimpsed his figure as it rushed into the bathroom, and she heard the shower turned on hard.

She lay on the bed, still naked, when he came out, using her beauty to strike out at him.

"Why did you marry me, Dirk?" she bit out. "Why?"

"Don't ask stupid questions," he said, lying down on the bed.

"It's not a stupid question," she shot back. She felt his hand against her cheek. "Everything in time, darling," he said. "My way, remember?" He turned over and went to sleep, and she was alone in bed with her husband, but she was alone, more alone than she'd ever been in her life. Was this beautiful stranger next to her a sadist? Or did he really have a plan for some explosion of ecstacy? She went to sleep unsure, unanswered, and unfulfilled.

But he did have a plan, she was to learn, a plan that he carried through with consummate skill. Her life continued to be a thing of hopes offered and whisked away, days of tenderness and solicitude, and nights of coldness. Some mornings, before leaving for work, he would go over her body and hold out promise for the night. But the night always brought his long walks and nothing more. She was becoming more and more depressed, she knew. Only later, much later, did she come to realize that his long walks made certain he was safe from being aroused by her beauty. Then, one night, she fell upon him again but this time he slapped her—hard—and she felt fear. It was a few nights later when she spoke to him as he lay beside her.

"You're killing me, Dirk," she said. "There'll be nothing left when you're ready."

"Nonsense," he had said curtly. She wanted to run, but there was no place to run. Her Aunt and Uncle had been deeply hurt by her runaway marriage. She couldn't go to them. Besides, she had too much pride for that. So she stayed and continued to wonder if her beautiful Dirk was a sadist to end all sadists. He seemed to be doing a wonderful job of it. If only he wouldn't alternate so between everything she wanted and everything she didn't want. He kindled her hopes so cleverly that she was like a dog that pants after food held in sight and sits patiently when it doesn't materialize, always hoping, waiting. Even her studies were nothing to her anymore, just empty motions. Then finally, one day, she decided that Dirk was sick. He needed help. It was a conclusion that somehow heartened her. It held a promise of action, of hope. She'd talk to him that night about going to see a psychiatrist.

She fixed martinis when he came home and sat down to tell him what she had decided, steeling herself against being turned aside by his charm and those deep, luminous eyes. But once again he surprised her and once again she knew how much she loved him. "Maybe you're right," he had said. "I'll do it. I'll make an appointment tomorrow." Renewed hope sprang in her at once. He understood. He really did. She could wait longer, now that she'd caught at a ray of hope. She went to sleep that night happier than she'd been on any night since they'd married.

He came home the next day eager to tell her of his first visit to the psychiatrist, a doctor Edmondson. Dirk described the doctor, his offices, and everything about his hour. The doctor's first recommendation was for them to get out more with other couples. Nancy couldn't see how that would help matters with Dirk, but she certainly knew little of the workings of the human psyche, and so she was happy to go along with the plan. Dirk began arranging get-togethers almost every weekend with couples from his office, young couples like themselves. He always planned some fun activity. He planned it all so very well.

There was that first time, at the beach, when he urged Nancy to swim across the long inlet with Caroline who had been an Olympic swimmer. Nancy balked. "I'm not that strong a swimmer, Dirk," she had said to him quietly. But he'd insisted, urging her on, telling her she could do it easily. "Do it for me, darling, for us," he said. "Everyone's watching. I've told them all how you could do anything. Don't disappoint me." He was a little boy, pleading, his deep eyes telling her the things she wanted to see in them. She gave in and started the long swim with the other girl. She was half-way across the inlet when she felt her strength give way. It happened suddenly, her muscles just giving out and she felt herself go under. She had no strength to fight back. It would have been the end had the other girl not glanced back and turned at once to swim back and keep her afloat.

Later that night, Dirk held her and apologized to her for urging her into it. Exhausted, she was content just to be in his arms and go to sleep.

It was the very next weekend when they were at the amusement park with two other couples from the store that Dirk insisted she go with a few of the others to the very top of the Space Tower, a swaying needlelike structure designed to simulate the thrills of an imaginary space platform.

"But I can't stand heights," she had whispered to him. "I get all tensed and dizzy." But once more he teased and coaxed and shamed her into going, wheedling and charming her, and she agreed. But only if he'd hold onto her. On the top of the tower, a swaying, circular platform with a thin rail around it, she grew faint and dizzy at once. But she clung to Dirk with one hand and the small railing with the other. The others were laughing, and sometimes the girls would scream when a gust of wind made the tower tilt precariously. She could only stand still with every muscle tensed, fighting off the waves of dizzy nausea. Suddenly Dirk pulled away from her and went around to the other side of the platform. "Be right back, pet," she heard him say. She grabbed to stop him but he was gone. The tower swayed, the dizziness turned into blackness, and she felt herself falling, collapsing. There was a wide space beneath the single railing, wide enough for someone on the floor to roll through and off. Her body rolled under it and somebody, a stranger she learned later, caught her and pulled her back. She only wakened after they'd brought her back down to the ground.

That night, Dirk made light of the incident. He replaced his tender solicitude of the previous week with a we-won't-talk-about-it air. But Nancy was bothered, deeply bothered by it. He had twice now urged her into something she hadn't wanted to do, something which had almost been tragically fatal. And the nights continued with his long walks and then the stranger beside her in bed, the ache of her body, the emotional desperation she felt. But in between, he would tell her of his visits to Dr. Edmondson, and she clung to that hope. Alone in the night, she kept thinking of how she'd almost been killed at Dirk's urging, how his silly, foolish, childish insistence had almost brought death to her. How childish was it really, she heard the dark question asked in the back of her mind. She turned it off at once, shocked and horri-fied at her own sick thoughts. But it was the very next weekend when she grew sick at her own dark mind once again. Dirk had arranged a get-together with the same group at a lake where one of the girls had a family summer home, complete with speedboat and water skiing facilities.

Nancy had only water skied once and hadn't liked it that much. The speed and centrifugal force involved tended to make her dizzy, as heights made her dizzy. But Dirk insisted again that she ski, and this time he grew petulant as she balked. All the other girls had done it and he wanted her to be as good as they were, certainly to show that his wife was as good a sport as the others. She continued to resist and finally, taking her side, he pleaded again. "Dr. Edmondson says it's important for me to have pride in you," he confessed, almost shamefully. That did it. She melted and agreed. "I'll drive the boat for you," Dirk said. "I'll keep watching you."

She put on the water skiis and the speedboat took off, Dirk at the wheel. She felt the speed increase at once. Dirk glanced back and she shook her head vigorously, telling him to slow down. He was steering in a tight circle and she felt the pull of the centrifugal force against her and the dizziness starting to come over her. "Dirk!" she screamed, but the wind only blew her cry back into her teeth. He glanced back again, too quickly to catch her eye it seemed, and she was unable to wave, clinging to the line with both hands. She was feeling herself go out of control. The speedboat swung her sharply, and Dirk opened the throttle wider. There was a long wooden pier coming up, jutting out into the lake. He was swinging her around, dangerously close to it. Then suddenly the boat hit a wave or something for she saw Dirk turn the wheel sharply. The shock wave hit the long line, traveling back down to her with gathering force. She felt the shock of it upset her balance. The speed of the swing did the rest, and she was suddenly shooting off like a stone ricocheted from a speeding car. The wooden pier was just to the right, her body hurtling into it. She closed her eyes as she slammed sideways against it. But miraculously, astonishingly, there was no final, killing, shattering crash. She felt herself hit the water and she snapped her eyes open. Somehow she had missed the heavy wooden pilings, and her body had sailed through the narrow space—just wide enough for her to fit between them. She was in the water under the pier. She reached out, pulled herself forward against one and then arms were reaching down from the top of the pier, pulling her up and out of the water. She fainted when they got her on the pier and woke later on a cot in one of the lakeside homes.

Dirk took her home, then. It was nearly time to go, anyway. Her body hurt and she felt numb. But it was a numbness that went far deeper than her mere physical self. Home finally, she lay on the bed in the semidarkness, the dark, sickening, agonizing thoughts leaping in her mind. She couldn't turn them off anymore. She could only feel sick and ashamed and petrified for having them. But they persisted and she faced them now. There was no other place to look but at them. She was surprised she could voice her thoughts, her voice as numbed and drained of emotion as she was.

"Are you trying to kill me, Dirk?" she asked hollowly.

"That's not even sick humor," he said. "That's just plain, ordinary bad taste."

"So is trying to kill someone," she said and turned over. He didn't bring it up in the morning and he left without speaking to her. Once alone, her thoughts tumbled about wildly, almost uncontrollably, and she felt her body grow cold and hot and cold again as she paced the bedroom, trembling. Is this how you begin a nervous breakdown, she wondered? Dirk had brought her near to it emotionally, and now perhaps his sadism wasn't enough any longer. Perhaps now it had turned to something more final. But what could she do? How do you go up to a policeman and say, policeman, sir, my husband, my beautiful, handsome Dirk, is trying to kill me? He'd ask her what made her think so, and she'd tell him of a lot of foolish incidents that had happened. It would all be ridiculous in his eyes, in anyone else's eyes. They couldn't know how he'd killed her slowly ever since their wedding night. They couldn't be expected to fit all the pieces together as only she could. They might even say she was paranoid. She stopped her pacing. Maybe they would be right. Maybe she was. Maybe she'd been brought to that.

Suddenly she thought of the doctor whom Dirk had been seeing, the psychiatrist. She'd go to him and talk to him herself. If anyone could understand, he'd be the one. She dressed quickly and looked up Dr. Edmondson in the phone book. She got an appointment only by pleading with the nurse and promising it would be short. She was scheduled to see him at the very end of his day, six-thirty. She got there at six and waited. The office was just as Dirk had described it, and so was Dr. Edmondson.

Dirk was home when she returned, drinking a martini. The heat rose up from the street ten stories below, and she went into the cool darkness of the bedroom, raised the window fully and sat on the edge of the sill letting the air blow against her. Dirk came to the doorway, the martini in his hand, watching her.

"What's the matter, pet?" he asked softly.

"What is it all for, Dirk?" Nancy answered, not looking at him. "What kind of torture are you trying to put me through? Are you trying to drive me mad?" She had almost said "kill me" but she had put aside those hideous thoughts for now. The rest was horrible enough without wrestling with that finality.

"Christ, Nancy, don't start that again," Dirk said disgustedly. "Get a hold of yourself."

"I went to see Doctor Edmondson today," Nancy said, still looking out the window into the night, perched on the sill. There was silence and she turned to look at Dirk. A small, wry smile tinged the beautiful face, and the deep, luminous eyes stared back at her. He put the martini down atop the dresser.

"The doctor told me you'd only been to see him once and had never come back," she said slowly. "All those stories about your talks with him, they were all lies, pure lies."

She heard her voice, calm, measured, and almost laughed at it because inside her there was a terrible tearing, shredding, ripping going on. She looked at Dirk again, her beautiful Dirk, just standing there, watching her. The world lay broken at his feet, her world, everything that mattered to her. It all lay there in pieces

and she lay there with it, in as many pieces. Poor Dirk, she said
to herself. He just stood there, those beautiful eyes watching her,
that wry smile on his lips, his chin lifted in that arrogant way
of his. Only now he seemed a defiant little boy. She wondered if
he knew himself why he had done this to them, to her. He had
wanted to torture her—that was obvious—to emotionally and
psychologically torture her. He'd made up the psychiatrist's visits
because it kept her hopes up, and he could laugh at his own cunning. And he had been cunning. He'd been able to do it because
he'd first made her worship him totally, completely.

But she didn't ask him anything. There would only be more
lies. She looked away, out of the window, across the rooftops, the
houses where millions of people lived and none so shattered as
she. Her insides were still tearing apart, and she was feeling sick.
There was a sudden movement and she turned to glance at Dirk.
Her eyes widened and her lips opened to scream but she couldn't.
Horror had frozen her voice. He was rushing at her, headlong,
hands outstretched to push her out of the window. And he was
smiling, a coldly triumphant smile. Finally the scream came, one
word *"Dirk!"*

She twisted away, slipped, and fell back into the room. She
felt her shoulders hit him at the knees, felt him trip over her,
and the next thing was the scream, the agonizing, wavering
scream that tore from him as he plunged through the window.
She grasped the sill and looked out as his body fell through
the night, and she thought, wildly, incongruously, even now
he's so graceful. But the darkest, most hideous of her thoughts
had been right. He had tried to kill her those other times when
it would seem only a tragic accident. And just now, it would
have been another accident. She'd have fallen out the window. But all the time he had wanted her dead. Kneeling at the
window sill, she screamed down after the falling figure, only
a small shape below now. "Why, Dirk, why?" she screamed.
"Why, why?"

When the police came to the apartment she was still asking it, sitting on the floor, her eyes blank, spouting incoherent, senseless nothings. She was there but her mind was in a lost land of its own. All that had been unreal. Or was it the other way around? It didn't matter anymore, reality, unreality. It was all a hideous dream, as real as she had made it, as real as Dirk. Or was it as real as her shattered mind?

They took her away to a hospital, first, then to a big gray building. Edna and Max came to see her often and she spoke to them. She spoke to everyone, doctors, nurses, other patients. Only she spoke of nothing in strange sentences and laughed when they couldn't unravel the real meaning from the unreal one. But the nights were the worst part. Men would chase her, some wanting her, some only wanting to kill her, all with dark, luminous eyes. She would run through the corridors of white, screaming until the attendants caught her, and then she would hide in a corner until her pursuers finally went away. They, the attendants, the doctors and nurses, told her no one was chasing her, but there was someone real that wanted her. They just didn't know what was real and what wasn't.

And so, for a long time, there was no difference between the two for Nancy Hazleton. And best of all, she didn't want any difference. It was better this way. But then there was a succession of long talks with analysts and therapists. She didn't listen much to their big words such as trauma and conscious rejection. They amused her but didn't explain that "why" she still sought. Then a young doctor came and spoke to her in rough, everyday language and made her angry.

"You still don't want to let yourself believe that your darling husband wanted to kill you," he said. "But the fact is that he did."

"Why, dammit, why?" Nancy screamed at the young doctor, and it was her first direct remark since she had kneeled at that window and called after Dirk's falling body. The doctor had shrugged. "He was a madman," he said. "Whatever made him that way is something we'll never know. That's the only explanation and you better start to live with it."

She glared at the doctor but things started to get better after that. Oh, the endless sessions with analysts and therapists went on, but she listened and helped and finally she had a certain pride that her suspicions had been right all along. It helped her to know that once she had been able to distinguish reality from fancy. She had just refused to let herself see it.

She came to believe in herself once again, and the nights stopped being haunted by demons of the mind. She left the big gray building finally, stayed with Edna and Max again, and then returned to finish the last three months of school she had to complete. Returning to the apartment with all its memories was her major conquest outside the hospital but she had done it, redecorating the place from top to bottom, making it into something new. But mostly she conquered because she accepted the fact of her unanswered question staying unanswered. The reality that had threatened her life and the demons of her mind had been put away together. She had let go of the past.

And now, all of a sudden, the past had returned. The real and unreal had come back to haunt her once again.

# CHAPTER SIX

THE GIRL LAY STILL, UTTERLY DRAINED and wrung out by the story that was not just a story but a reliving of her life. She stared up at the ceiling and heard Peter Thatcher's voice, gentle, soft, and felt his hand pressing her shoulder.

"You poor kid," he said. "What a horrible experience." Nancy sat up and swung her long, lovely legs from the bed.

"Now you know everything," she said, bitterness in her tone. "And now what do you think, Peter? Am I mad?"

Peter's hands were on her shoulders and he turned her to face him, looking deeply into her eyes.

"Nonsense," he said. "You had an experience that would unhinge any girl, and some permanently. Now you've come here on this job and had a run of plain rotten luck, a chain of circumstances that, for you, have been terribly disturbing. There was that first night which I still say happened pretty much the way I figured it did. Your imagination, bigger and better than most people's, anyway, just took off. Then you have the rotten luck to meet a girl with eyes that remind you of the past. Nerves, tension, memory, it all combines to make the past come alive again, to trigger a temporary attack of your old fears. And remember, they're not so very old."

Peter saw the stubborn, set line of Nancy's jaw, the doggedness mirrored in her eyes. "You won't accept that, will you?" he said to her.

"I can't," she said flatly. "Don't you see, I can't? I was right all along that last time, right from my very first disappointed suspicions. I wouldn't allow myself to believe it. But I was right. That was the terrible part of it. I'd give anything to have been wrong, even about a little piece of it. There are times when it's a terrible thing to be right. But I was."

"And so you still believe there was an abandoned house grown over by the forest, a sub-human creature, and signs on an old railroad station, even though you saw they weren't there for yourself."

"Yes," she said defiantly. "They were real. I have to believe that, don't you see, Peter?"

"But the nightmares in the sanatorium, you told me yourself that they were real to you at the time, too," Peter countered. "But you know now they were all creatures of your own making."

Nancy fought down the tears she felt rising in her eyes. Of course he was right, that was the awful part about it. What was real and what was not? Could she admit she wasn't sure? Dare she admit that? Or would that hasten the process of unraveling?

"All you have to do, Nancy, is put a damper on your imagination," Peter went on. "Refuse to let your mind run away with you, and all your fears will go away. Give it a try."

She saw the sincerity in his hazel eyes.

"It's not that simple, Peter," she said. "There are more things I just can't explain, not even as fantasies." She went on to tell him of how she seemed to know just where the kitchen was at Bloodroots and the steps to the basement.

"Am I mad, Peter?" she said sadly. "I mean, really mad? They say the mad have powers other people don't. What does it all mean?"

His arms were holding her suddenly. "I can't tell you what that means, Nancy," he said. "But you're not mad. You're upset and still suffering deep emotional and mental wounds, that's all."

"I don't know," she said, shaking her head. "Maybe it's just fate, then. Sometimes I think some people and some families are just touched by an evil star. Misfortune seems to dog them all the time. There was my mother and father, killed in that freak accident when I was five. I was told that mother had escaped being killed a number of times before in weird accidents. Then her mother, my grandmother, died in childbirth. There was talk that she'd run away from home when she was near to giving birth and very upset about something. Anyway, she died in childbirth. It seems a chain of misfortune and maybe I'm just the latest in the chain."

Peter shook her gently. "You stop that kind of talk," he said. Suddenly his warm, soft lips were on hers and his hands held her and she felt their warm strength on her naked body under the thin cotton shirt. She felt her blood surge, her arms circle him, her lips answering. Finally he let her go, and she knew that not since those first days with Dirk had she felt like this.

"You just try doing what I said," Peter commanded. "Stop making yourself paranoid. Stop seeing dark shadows in everything that happens. Stop thinking everything is an attempt on your life."

"Like what happened just now at Rock Lake," Nancy said.

"Exactly," Peter said.

"I'll try," Nancy said. "You're pretty wonderful, Peter, just to listen to me about all this."

"Listening to you is as nice a thing as I can think of doing," he grinned down at her. "Come on, I'll see you back. I'll show you a shortcut through the woods from here to the manor. You can use it next time you want to come see me. The other way along the roads is damn long walking."

He had her by the arm and was guiding her outside and up the small hill behind the cabin, into the woods along a narrow trail. It was a lovely little path, speckled by the sun as it trickled its way through the thick leaves overhead.

"How is your work coming, Peter?" she asked as they walked along together. What she silently asked was how long would he still be here in the Little Smokies after she left. And with Jodie solicitously taking care of him. But she didn't dare put those thoughts into words. Not yet, anyway.

"Things are coming along very well," Peter said. "I've catalogued an amazing amount of data on the origins and migration of these people. Of course there are holes. There are always holes in this sort of thing, gaps you just can't fill, families who've died away. Though in areas such as this one, unchanging, insular, genealogically undiluted, so to speak, that's sort of unusual. There's one here, the Cragsheads, who apparently just up and vanished. There are some tombstone markers over a hundred years old but nothing else. Oh, and I interviewed one nearly deaf old man who told me old stories of the Cragshead family as being a violent group, very much feared."

"What about the Howells?" Nancy asked.

"They're one of the oldest families here," he said. "The original Howells were also the most industrious and apparently built up an outside income while they constructed Bloodroots. Of course, I've gathered all this from old records I dug up and some filed land grants. There's really not much else to go on. Except songs and they're important mostly in tracing migration patterns."

Peter paused and then cast a sly little look at Nancy. "Actually, I ought to be finished with my work here pretty soon."

She felt her cheeks color. "Do you read minds, too?" she laughed.

"No, just girls," he grinned. The path opened a little suddenly and there, ahead, she saw Bloodroots. The path was ending at the end of the line of trees just opposite her room. Peter stopped short of the end. "You go on," he said. "The less talk the better." She understood. Or she thought she did. But she couldn't help wondering, the eternal female in her, if he hadn't been specifically thinking about not seeing Jodie. No matter. The touch of his lips on hers was still with her and she was glad, herself, that no one was around as she hurried across the grass to the house, slipped inside, and raced up to her room. She changed into a simple, light dress and went back downstairs. Samuel Howell was just entering from the back of the house as she was finishing a sketch in the living room, one she was happy with, and she showed it to him.

"I'd have had more done but I took Jodie's suggestion about taking a swim in that little Rock Lake," she told the big man as he admired the design. When she went on to tell him what had happened she saw his eyes fix on her, growing darker, angrier as she went into the incident deeper. She had just finished, and Samuel Howell's face was a frowning mass of folds when Jodie came in. The girl stopped, seeing Nancy, her face blanching, her jaw dropping.

"You ... you're all right," she gasped. "You're alive."

"You heard what happened?" Nancy asked.

"Zachary heard someone opened the sluice gates, and I knew I'd told you to go up there for a swim. I thought the worst."

"It was just one of those accidents," Nancy said and saw Samuel Howell's eyes holding Jodie in a burning stare. The folds of his jowls trembled. Was it just that he was upset? Or was it anger? Nancy couldn't be sure.

"I was going to tell you I'd sent Miss Nancy up there," Jodie said to her father. "Honest I was, Pa."

Samuel Howell's eyes continued to hold his daughter for what seemed an endless moment, and then Nancy saw him win the struggle to compose himself as he turned to her.

"Jodie knows I don't like her or Cassie to swim up there," he said, managing a small smile for Nancy. "She knows I wouldn't want her to send you, our guest and our responsibility, up there."

It was a reasonable explanation of his anger, Nancy decided, and certainly fitted in with what Peter had said about the other times the sluice gates had been opened. Why did she continue to sense that there was more to his deep fury over the incident. And there was more to it, she was certain. But she refused to let herself speculate about it, remembering Peter's admonition about seeing dark shadows behind everything.

Nancy murmured a few more things about not holding Jodie to blame and went to her room. From the top of the stairway she saw Jodie leave the living room, too, going to the east wing of the house. Dinner that night was underlain with tensions, and she noticed that Cassie seemed to be enjoying the fact that Jodie was in bad graces. Nancy was glad when dinner ended and she could go back to her roon. She worked there, polishing her sketches, doing finished drawings of her ideas for designing the living room, pleased with what she finally had when she went to bed.

She lay in the dark and thought of Peter, letting nice, warm thoughts fill her mind for a change. She wouldn't have heard Jodie and her father fighting if she hadn't forgotten to bolt her door and gotten up to do so. Opening the door for a moment to close it properly, she heard the angry voices from downstairs in the living room, first Jodie's, bitter, cutting, even more so than it had been that night with Cassie beneath the window.

"You're not taking this away from me," Jodie said. "It's my right to do."

"Damn it is," Samuel Howell boomed. "You'll do what I tell you to do. It's got to be done my way, without any loose ends."

" 'Less you promise me what I want, I'm going to do it when I get the chance," Jodie replied, and Nancy heard the older Howell's roar, followed by the sound of a hard slap and then another.

"Damn you, girl," the man's voice thundered. "You stay clear of this. You keep your mouth shut and don't try anything like that again. There's been too much planning gone into this to have you bungle it at the last minute. It's too important to us all."

Nancy heard Jodie run from the room. "Then you better promise me, Pa, you better," she heard the girl fling back and the sound of her footsteps faded away into the other part of the house. Nancy bolted the door and went back to bed. What was to be done Samuel Howell's way, she wondered? What was Jodie to keep her mouth shut about? What wasn't she to try again? What had she bungled and might do so again? The things Nancy had heard had all been cryptic, and a terrible uneasiness stirred inside her. She kept thinking of how Samuel Howell had become so angered and disturbed over Jodie sending her to swim at Rock Lake. Somehow, she felt certain this fight had something to do with that. But what? Again, dark thoughts started to slip into her mind but she turned them away, pushing them into a corner, hearing Peter's words. "Stop seeing dark shadows behind everything." Nancy made herself turn over and go to sleep on those words and somehow managed to sleep the whole night through.

In the morning, after breakfasting alone, she went outside. She had pushed aside dark thoughts, but she'd also found that you can't push away the mind's need to know, to be reassured. Cassie was in her herb garden behind the house, she saw, as she passed. Jodie was there, too, holding a dress and blouse in her hands. Both Jodie and Cassie had their backs to her as she hurried past but their words came through the quiet morning air. "Dammit you've been into my things again," Jodie was saying. "If you don't stop I'll fix you, Cassie."

"You never told me about the other night," Cassie said, petulance in her voice. "You tell me and I'll leave your things alone."

Nancy walked on and the voices faded from her hearing. She went up the grassy slope, over the ridge, and to the little path by the birches that led to Rock Lake. The lake was its former self again, crystal clear and sparkling, but the ground she walked was wet and squishy underfoot. She circled the lake, moving past it, climbing up towards the tall rocks where the sluice gates, now shut, allowed a small trickle of water to splash down. It was a steep climb, but she found a kind of trail amid the rocks and finally was at the top. Hard, scraggly, scrub brush grew there, mostly mountain brush such as ground hemlock and ephedra and a few twisted oaks here and there. Nancy walked to the sluice gates, and saw the handles that were attached to them, running on long metal rods to the rocks. Behind the gates was the big mountaintop lake that fed the clear water down into the small man-made lake below. It was, indeed, not at all hard to open the sluices, she saw and she wondered just why she had felt the need to come up here and see for herself. But she had wanted to, from the very moment she woke up. She also had found herself thinking of the argument between Jodie and Samuel Howell last night and the strange uneasiness was still inside her. She'd try to get down to see Peter again later, she decided. Just being with the tall, rangy, hazel-eyed man made her feel at ease, more safe and secure, somehow.

She turned and started down the steep pathway from the top again. She brushed past the hard leaves of one of the ephedra that grew out over the pathway. Her skirt caught and she felt it start to tear and halted at once, carefully disengaging it from the branches of the bush. It was then that she saw the little square of yellow and red cloth caught on one of the bushes right alongside. Nancy reached into the bush and pulled it out. It was rayon, a torn piece of a girl's dress. She felt her heart skip, felt the dark thoughts leap at once. It was a piece torn from a dress, unquestionably. And it had a print pattern of red lines on a yellow background. It would be easy enough to match, she noted grimly. Nancy put the piece into the pocket of her skirt and started down the path again, suspicion and wonder and anger filling her mind. Don't see shadows, she repeated to herself. But this time she held her own answer to that. Maybe she wasn't seeing shadows. Maybe she was seeing something else and this time she wouldn't refuse to look as she'd refused those times with Dirk. She couldn't refuse to look, not and keep any belief in herself. She thought of the deserted old station and the signs that weren't there. If she were wrong again, she would realize it and be strengthened for it. Knowing was something that could only help her, even knowing she was seeing dark shadows, making up demons again.

She finally arrived back at Bloodroots and worked the rest of the day with a grim determination that made her pencil fly and somehow sparked her creatively. She got a lot done and was exhausted when the night finally came. She'd decided against going to see Peter. She'd only still think about what she hadn't found out yet. She'd wait till she knew, then she could go to him, one way or the other. Samuel Howell was delighted with the finished drawings she showed him for the dining room and he kept them to go over with Jodie and Cassie. Over dinner she tactfully pressed Jodie about her plans for the evening and took her own answer out of Jodie's casual evasiveness. Jodie's evasive replies seemed to agitate Cassie, though, and Nancy was beginning to realize why. The older girl lived vicariously through Jodie. Twisted, dark threads ran through the Howells and apparently through this isolated, inverted valley. When dinner was over, Nancy went to her room, turned out the lights, and took up a position by the window. She waited patiently, and with her door slightly ajar, heard Samuel Howell finally leave the living room and retire to the other part of the house. She looked down the dark corridor to the barricaded door at the other end, and then bolted her own door and took up her position at the window again. She heard Cassie's voice, first, below the window, and then Jodie's.

"I knew you were going someplace when you got so cute at dinner," she heard Cassie say. "I'll tell Pa unless you promise to tell me about it later. Pa's plenty mad at you now, Jodie."

"Pa won't be mad at me for this," Jodie said. "And you keep your mouth shut, Cassie, or you won't get to hear anything ever."

Nancy saw Jodie walk across the grass, up toward the ridge, and then cut into the little pathway that led from Peter's cabin through the woods. Nancy fought down the instant desire to follow her there and interrupt whatever plans she had. But it was impossible. Nancy had plans of her own, plans she had to carry out first. She left the window and lay down on the bed and waited in the darkness. She let an hour go by and then opened the door of her room. She listened first, and then went out into the hallway, casting a quick glance down to the dark end. The house was silent and the lights were out below. Nancy slipped off her shoes and moved on bare feet silently down the stairs. She waited again at the bottom, listening, and then she tip-toed into the east wing of the big house. She heard the sound of Samuel Howell's deep, regular breathing come from one of the rooms—not quite a snore, yet a heavy, rasping sound. She went by the room, the door ajar, and up the east stairway. There was a sliver of light from beneath the first closed door and Nancy hurried past it. That would be Cassie's room, she guessed. She opened the door of the other room across the hall and went in. The room was like hers in layout and size, with the two big windows. Jodie's clothes were strewn about it carelessly.

Nancy moved among the girl's things, picking each piece of clothing up and examining it closely in the moonlight shining through the window. The small square of torn cloth in her pocket, she went to Jodie's closet. Jodie, she had already decided, was far from a neat girl. Things were draped and hung carelessly all over the room, and the closet was not much better. Few dresses were straight on their hangers, and some hangers held three and four things. It was a laborious task, taking each piece of clothing from the closet out into the room where the weak light shone from outside. Suddenly Nancy heard a sound, a door being opened. Footsteps came toward Jodie's room, and Nancy was suddenly grateful for Jodie's sloppy habits. She dropped the dress in her hands, hanger and all, on the floor and looked around wildly. She took the only course open, diving under the big bed, wriggling her body quickly to move deeper under it as she heard the door open.

The light went on in the room, one small lamp, but it was enough for Nancy to see Cassie's legs as the girl went to the closet. From her worm's-eye view under the bed she could see surprisingly well, particularly when Cassie went to the far side of the room where a mirror hung on the wall. Nancy watched as Cassie stepped out of her high-necked gray dress and put on a dress of Jodie's, leaving the buttons open almost down to her waist. Cassie was sharp-angled, her figure as wide and broad as Jodie's, but bigger-boned with no soft curves whatever. Cassie walked around the room in Jodie's clothes, smiling, humming to herself, playing her own imaginary roles in her own imaginary little dramas. She changed costume three times, sometimes turning and whirling to dance to music only she could hear. Nancy watched, sometimes getting a view only of the girl's feet as she whirled alongside the edge of the bed, other times seeing all of her as she went to the end of the room.

Nancy felt her skin wet with perspiration, and the dust of the floor under the bed was filling her nostrils. She moved a hand to cover her nose and breathed through her mouth. If she were caught, she would have no chance to explain, she was certain. Cassie had a rawboned strength to her, a cold, determined quality that was frightening. And seen in Jodie's things, her anger might be more than she could control, Nancy knew. But it was cramped under the bed, the springs digging into her back, the wood floor hard, hurting her breasts. Yet, she dared not move a muscle and make the bedsprings sound. She gritted her teeth as the perspiration ran down her nose, hanging on the end of her nostrils to drop finally. Even if Cassie didn't react violently, and Nancy could think up some hurried explanation, her purpose for coming to Jodie's room would be unaccomplished, and somehow she knew she'd never get another chance, particularly if her suspicions were right. So she stayed still, and her muscles cramped and grew tight, and she screamed silently in pain as they contracted into tight bundles of tension.

Finally, Cassie tired of her games. She put her own clothes back on, turned off the light and closed the door softly behind her. Nancy waited till she heard the sound of Cassie's door being closed before she crawled out from under the bed. She pulled herself to her feet by inches, every muscle crying out in pain, and she lay bent over the bed for a long time, letting her body stretch itself. Cassie had been there for hours, and she knew Jodie could return at any moment. Disregarding the pain, Nancy got to her feet and began to move clothes from the closet by the armful and then, suddenly, with a shocking impact, the yellow dress was there, the red print over the yellow base. Nancy took the piece of torn cloth from her skirt pocket, turned the dress over, and found the rip. The piece fitted perfectly, and Nancy's eyes were dark with fright and confusion as she put the dress back into the closet. She kept the piece of cloth in her pocket. Her mind raced with the terrible impact of what she had found. Jodie had been there, at the sluice gates, opening them, trying to kill her. It was Jodie who had suggested she go to Rock Lake for a swim and then had crept up to the sluice gates to open them, knowing Nancy would be swept to her death in the cascade of turbulent water. There was no rhyme or reason to any of it, but then there had been no rhyme or reason to Dirk, either. Was it her fate to be the victim of the mad, Nancy asked herself solemnly. Did Samuel Howell know of Jodie's madness? Or was he, too, involved? She thought of the statements she had heard them make during the angry argument. But there were only more unanswered questions there. She hadn't been seeing dark shadows, Nancy told herself. Her suspicions had again been right, she had the evidence in her pocket.

She went to the door, and opened it a crack to peer out. The hall was dark except for the sliver of light that came from beneath the door to Cassie's room. Nancy hurried past it and down the stairs, hoping she would not meet Jodie returning. She breathed easier when she reached the stairway at the end of the other side of the house and hurried up its blackness. Beside the door to her room she halted, peering down the inky black corridor to the far end. Then she moved forward gropingly, her hands feeling along the wall. The inky blackness of the hall refused to lighten even though her eyes had grown accustomed to the dark. Only when her legs bumped against the edge of the chairs did she know she was at the end of the hallway. She put her ear to the heavy wooden door and listened. Something or someone was inside. She could feel it and then she heard a sound, a shuffling on the other side of the door. Her hand moved toward the doorknob and then drew back. Her arms and legs were still cramped and she felt tired. The shuffling sound had stopped and Nancy moved from the door. She had done enough for this night. She had flirted enough with danger, and her heart was pounding again. She groped her way back to her room and bolted the door. Putting the skirt with the torn piece of dress on the lower corner of the bed, she undressed and went to the window. The night was cooler, and the mists hadn't risen to blanket the land. She was just about to turn from the window when she saw the figure moving out of the little pathway between the trees, Jodie's full, sensuous shape, and she watched the girl walk to the house and disappear from her line of vision.

With shocking suddenness, Nancy gasped silently. Was that it, she asked herself? Was Jodie Howell insanely jealous enough, warped and twisted enough to try to kill or injure her because of her visits to Peter? It was preposterous. It would be preposterous anywhere else. But in this land of feuds and vendettas with origins too unimportant to even remember, anything was believable. In this valley where outsiders were hated with an unfathomable, inwardly-turned, unbalanced sense of proportion, jealousy could assume strange shapes. It was not beyond belief and yet, as she lay between the sheets, it didn't satisfy her as an explanation. But she was experiencing something of jealousy herself as she thought of Jodie with Peter all evening. Apparently Peter Thatcher's hazel-eyed gentle kindness was something he dispensed quite freely, she sniffed. Well, tomorrow she'd have a few things to tell him about seeing shadows in everything. And maybe a few other things, too. She went to sleep, grateful in a way for the good, uncomplicated, old-fashioned jealousy that temporarily turned aside her dark fears.

# CHAPTER SEVEN

S HE ROSE EARLY AND WENT DOWNSTAIRS, pausing again to look down the corridor. The closed door stared back at her but she knew, now, in her own mind, that the room behind it was not empty. Samuel Howell had her finished drawings downstairs with him and had scrawled a few minor comments on them. The big man's huge face seemed even more massive this morning, the folds almost hiding the small blue eyes that watched her intently.

"You can begin preliminary work on the living room at once, Mr. Howell," Nancy said. "The window casements will have to be completely rebuilt to fit my designs. And the drapery will need to be ordered. Of course, I could do that for you when I return to the city."

"Yes, yes, I suppose so," Samuel Howell said, eyeing her. Nancy saw the man's reaction and knew he hadn't given any thought at all to the practical aspects of redecorating the big house. The fact surprised her and she felt herself frowning.

"Should I go on to the kitchen, and then Jodie and Cassie's rooms next?" she asked, and Samuel Howell nodded, breaking his heavy face into an expansive smile. "Why, yes, you just do that," he said. "That'll be fine. Meanwhile, I'll think about how we'll put these ideas of yours into action."

You just do that, Nancy almost mimicked, but she kept her lips shut and nodded politely. She had the skirt on with the torn bit of material in the pocket, and it burned against her skin. She left the big man and went outside, crossing quickly to the little path through the woods. She hurried down its speckled, cool trail, finally emerging at the rear of Peter's cabin. She saw Jed Batterbee stretching out on the grass at the side, and he rose up on one elbow as she came down past him.

"Morning, Jed," Nancy smiled at the slender, lithe figure, his guitar on the ground beside him. Jed nodded and the elfin little smile played across his lips. He plucked the guitar lazily with one finger. "Will ye go to the hieland wi' me, Lassie Lee?" he sang, and Nancy waved a hand at him as she went on.

"Perhaps later, Jed," she called back. Peter was packing tapes in a box and turned as Nancy appeared in the open doorway. His hazel eyes lighted at once, and Nancy forced herself not to rush forward into his arms. She made her eyes stay cool, steady.

"Have a nice evening last night?" she said and hated herself at once. It wasn't at all what she'd intended to say first. In fact, she hadn't intended to say it at all and now she had and her anger flared. Peter was regarding her calmly.

"Pleasant enough," was all he said.

"I see I'm not the only one you've shown that shortcut to your place here," Nancy said, again hating how inane she sounded and again unable to find the right words, the cool, controlled words.

"I don't think anyone has to show Jodie anything about the trails around these hills," Peter commented, and Nancy's lips tightened. His gentle admonishment had hit its target.

"I'm sorry, Peter," she said, crossing over to him. "But I'm upset, I guess. I've something to show you."

She took out the piece of torn cloth and told him of her climb to the sluice gates and then her visit to Jodie's room in the night. She told him of the argument she'd overheard between Jodie and her father, of the strangely mysterious remarks, and when she finished she saw the sternness of his eyes.

"I thought you promised to stop letting your imagination run away with you," Peter said.

"This isn't my imagination," Nancy said, shaking the piece of cloth under his nose. "I was right, don't you see?"

"No, I don't see that," Peter said and now there was impatient anger in his voice. "But I see you seem determined to fit things to your preconceived ideas."

"Preconceived ideas?" Nancy protested angrily. "How much evidence do you want, Peter?"

"Has it ever occurred to you that Jodie probably goes up on the trail to the big lake ten times a month perhaps?" Peter asked. "Maybe more? She could have gone up there a few days ago and torn her dress or even last week. All that torn piece you have there proves is that Jodie was up there and that's certainly not unusual."

Nancy felt the sting of his logic, the bitter reason of his words, but she couldn't let go so shamefully. "What about the argument?" she bit out. "What was Jodie told not to try again?"

"I don't know, Nancy," Peter said. "But they could have been arguing about a thousand different things, family matters, maybe something she tried to do to Cassie. There's no love lost between them. You've probably realized that. But it wasn't necessarily about you, and nothing you've told me or shown adds up to anything concrete. You're trying to find things to back up your imagination. You won't see that what you've come up with just doesn't make a case. You're not helping yourself that way, Nancy."

Nancy felt her cheeks red and not just with anger. Everything he said was plausible, reasonable. She couldn't deny that inside. Yet she couldn't deny how she felt, either, that cold, illogical fear that had taken hold of her. Dirk had had plausible answers for everything, too, she remembered only too well. His replies could turn aside her suspicions with smooth logic. And now Peter, with his investigative, analytical mind, was applying reason where she applied the senses. Reason, Nancy snorted silently, here in this land where there was little rational reason for anything that went on. But of course there was reason in his answers, validity to his questions. She'd wanted excited agreement, and he'd given her polite skepticism—smooth logic instead of sympathy. Anger and hurt governed her immediate reactions.

"I'm sorry I bothered you," she said icily. "I won't do it again until I've something convincing, like a bullet hole in me."

She turned and strode from the cabin, hearing him call after her but not turning. She wouldn't even take his short-cut but stalked off up the red dust of the road.

"I'll be here whenever you want me, Nancy," she heard him call to her, but she refused to look back and made herself wonder if he were so logical and analytical with Jodie. Hardly, she sniffed. Jodie wasn't the type for logic. Well, neither was she, Nancy muttered to herself. Maybe everything he'd pointed out was true, maybe everything she felt was fraught with other possible explanations. Yet, she held the feeling deeply inside her and she would continue to cling to it. Still, as she slowed her pace, she had to ask herself the deflating, depressing questions. Was she only being stubborn? Because she had been right once, did that make her forever wise? She had just reached a turn in the road when the slender, blond figure appeared atop a flat rock that peeked out from the wall of trees. He beckoned to her and she went toward him, watching him drop from sight for a moment as he sprang down from the rock. But he was waiting for her in a wooded clearing, his light, light eyes of opaque blue watching her with an expression she'd not seen there before, a kind of softness. But his small elfin smile was there, somehow reassuring in its constancy. He turned and led her to where a small stream magically appeared, tumbling its way through the cool woods, skipping along like a child at play. Jed sat down and Nancy sank to the soft mountain fern moss.

"I suppose you think I'm all wrong, too," Nancy said. "Or don't you know what Peter and I have argued about?"

Jed shrugged and she didn't know whether the shrug was in answer to her first or her second statement. He picked up the guitar and began to sing in the very sweetest, softest voice she had ever heard him use. The sun fell across his blond hair, curling in rings down the back of his neck as he sat cross-legged, only the open vest over the smooth, slenderness of his chest. The little dell grew silent as his voice rang out, and she saw a wood-thrush hop to a low branch to listen. A finch joined it and the wood and Jed and even she were transformed into a mythical moment when the boy-man-god Pan played to the nymphs and dryads of the mountainside. His voice, soft as a muted bell, clear as the mountain stream, caressed her.

> *"Do you happen to know of a maiden in need,*
> *Of a sweetheart to one who is anxious to plead,*
> *It's a shame that a handsome young fellow like me,*
> *Should be left while the nightingale sings in the tree,*
> *It's a shame that a handsome young fellow like me,*
> *Should be left while the nightingale sings in the tree.*
> *In the wood and the meadow beneath the bright moon,*
> *Every lad with his lass makes the most of the June,*
> *The world's gone a-wooing, excepting of me,*
> *And the nightingale sings to his mate in the tree,*
> *The world's gone a-wooing excepting of me,*
> *And the nightingale sings to his mate in the tree."*

When he finished he fell silent and gazed at the girl from beneath half-lowered eyes. Nancy reached out impulsively and put her hand over Jed's.

"Thank you, Jed," she said softly. "I know what you've tried to tell me in your way and I'm very touched by it. And very grateful. I wish I could say what I want to say as delicately as you've spoken to me but I can't. I'm not for you, Jed. I'm from that world outside, a world so very different."

Jed's eyes had lifted and their opaque lightness gazed at her and the soft smile seemed somehow sadder. She wondered if she were getting through to him. Did his fey, elfin, other-world self allow for such practical concepts as she was trying to bring forth. "I couldn't live here, Jed," she said. "And you'd hate my world. We wouldn't fit anywhere together. We must go a-wooing in our own worlds. Do you understand what I'm saying?"

Jed's smile didn't change but he spoke in that soft, cadenced speech pattern that was his.

"Maybe I do," he said. "But I like to make believe. I like to make my pictures of the mind and make believe they're real. I only make nice ones."

He got up abruptly, held out his hands and pulled her to her feet. She followed him through the woods as he led her on still another short-cut back to Bloodroots Manor. But his words stayed with her and she wondered: had she been making her own pictures of the mind, pictures that were the opposite of Jed's nice ones? Was the strangely tender, warm feeling she had for this boy-man just her own empathetic nature or did she relate to him because of the instinctive bond between those just outside the normal? The past was closing in on her again, the real and the unreal presenting themselves again for her to sort out, and she was glad to get to her room inside the manor house. Jed waved at her as she looked back from the doorway, and then she lay down in the room and let her mind stop its whirling. She would hurry and finish the rest of her designs here and leave, she decided. If Peter were right, if it were this place that had somehow triggered the past into haunting her again, then she'd free herself by leaving it. She'd finish and leave it to Samuel Howell, Jodie, and the others to put her work into actual being. Why had the huge man given that so little thought, she wondered again, the question flashing through her mind. Angrily, she snapped it off. She wouldn't pursue those enigmas, those riddles which led her only to one dark place. She got up, took her sketch pad, and went downstairs to the kitchen. The woman who came in the late afternoon to do the cooking was at work there, but Nancy ignored her and plunged into sketching, letting work absorb all her thoughts and energies. She finished two good design ideas for the kitchen and left them with Samuel Howell and excused herself for dinner. Her stomach was tight, the result of her working under self-pressure and all the other inner tensions she had gathered to herself. She took some tea and cornbread up to her room, stripped to bra and panties, and relaxed in the dark. The night had turned sultry and stifling again, and the song of a nightingale drifted up to her open window. She thought of Jed and his lovely, sweet love-song to her. And of course, Peter swam into her mind. She would go down and apologize to him in the morning. She knew she wanted very much to see him when he was through with his work and gone from here. But would he want to see her, she wondered. His lips on hers had seemed to say so but that, she knew, could only be her own hopes once again trying to make things fit what she wanted them to be. Dammit, it was habit that permeated everything, she realized in anger.

She got up, went to the door to bolt it, and glanced out into the hall at a sound, opening the door a crack. The man Zachary was there, coming back from the dark barricaded end of the corridor, a metal dish, the kind a dog eats out of, in his hands. She closed and locked the door quickly but she knew he had seen her peer out. She thought of the sounds she'd heard from behind that locked door last night, the shuffling and the chains. Did the Howells keep some huge dog back there, some fierce guard dog they let out only in the deep of the night. The man came running along the ridge that night and the creature chasing him, she saw it again in the swirl of the mists. The mists were already rising again tonight from the hot, steaming ground, as the night air drew them up in a huge natural cauldron. If Peter had been right, if nothing here really purposely touched her, this was still no place for her. There were too many strange, haunting things to urge her imagination into frightening, fearsome paths. She would try to be finished with the last of the designs by the end of the week. Of course, she'd have to get an additional sum from

Samuel Howell to pay train fare but that should pose no problem. She would be done with her part of the contract and the money would be due her.

Nancy undressed and lay naked on top of the bed, letting the night air cool her body. The breeze blew through the window in small, fitful gusts, as though it were rationing its gift. The room at the end of the inky hallway outside kept intruding into her thoughts, pulling at her, urging her to get up and go to the doorway again, perhaps to open it and see what lay behind it. The strength of the urge told her it was something more than idle curiosity that pulled her on. But she forced herself to lie still, to turn away from the desire. She made herself go to sleep by blanking out her conscious mind, a feat she'd mastered during the long months at the sanatorium. But the subconscious mind stayed awake and she slept with restless, disoriented visions of sub-human creatures chasing her, of an old fright of a house, of cascading water and death pulling at her. Yet she continued to remain physically asleep until the night exploded with gunfire and she sat up, eyes wide, startled. There were more shots and she heard shouting outside. She threw on a shift and ran to the window, peering out into the night mists.

Figures were running along the ridge, and she heard shots again. They were coming down toward the house, appearing and disappearing through the vapors, and then she heard the sound of Samuel Howell's voice outside, saw the stream of light from the windows downstairs reach out with yellow shafts. She heard Cassie, and Jodie, too. Nancy opened the door of her room and went downstairs. She almost used the side door but remembered that she was not to know that much about the old house. She went out the front door and around to the side, beneath her window. The mists had lifted a little and now she saw the running figures—halting, shirtless—trouser-clad men with rifles, gaunt, bearded, deep-eyed men. Jodie stood to one side with Cassie, and Nancy walked up just behind the two sisters.

"What in damn's goin' on, Seth?" she heard Samuel Howell ask the first man.

"Someone sneaking through the hollow," the man answered. "Billy saw him, couldn't nail him and sounded the alarm."

"One of the Gormans?" Samuel Howell said.

"Can't say. Maybe," the man called Seth answered. "They know enough to stay out of Wolf Hollow, though."

So that was it, Nancy realized. These were the Ordways, keepers of Wolf Hollow. But why did they look to Samuel Howell for directions, she wondered, and then she recalled that Peter had said the Ordways seemed to have some sort of an arrangement with Samuel Howell, "wards of a medieval Lord," he had called them.

"Did he get in deep, whoever it was?" the big man asked.

"No," Seth Ordway said. Nancy saw the man wipe the side of his face with a long hand and she gasped. There, just back of the thumb, was a huge purplish strawberry-shaped mark. Nancy felt her throat go dry. But Seth Ordway certainly wasn't the sub-human, demoniacal creature that had tried to kill her that first night in the storm. But the sight of the mark made it all return with renewed force. Nancy stepped back silently, against the deep shadows of the wall of the house. None of them had seen her, they'd been so involved in their own thoughts. She stayed flattened against the wall and heard the throbbing of her temples. She had almost been ready to dismiss the primordial beast as having come from her mind but now that terrible, chilling certainty seized her again. If she had been right all along about the creature, about the signs on the old station, about the flooding of the little lake, then she was in terrible danger. Maybe the unexplainable gaps were explainable, only not without the key. But did this strawberry mark on Seth Ordway's hand really prove anything? She stood there, hearing only seething questions again and no answers. What did it all mean? Was there a madness here? Was she an intended victim or someone who'd fallen into a bottomless pit quite by accident? Or was she once again letting her mind run away with itself?

More figures came running out of the night mists. "He came this way, over the ridge," one said.

"Keep searching," Samuel Howell commanded, his voice cold. "You've got enough men with you. Close a noose around the ridge and those woods over there, if you're sure he came this way."

"We're sure of that," the one man said. They turned and trotted off, and she heard their voices in the night, exchanging terse comments. Samuel Howell turned and started back into the house. "Get inside," he said curtly to Jodie and Cassie. "I don't like this one damn bit. I think maybe I've got to do some arranging instead of waitin' for the right time."

"I'm goin' to do it, Pa, don't forget that," Jodie said. Nancy saw the elder Howell pause just before they rounded the corner of the house, and glower at his daughter.

"You'll do what I told you to do and nothin' else," he thundered. "You interfere again and I'll beat the skin right off you."

There was no answer from Jodie, and they disappeared around the corner out of sight. Nancy heard the front door close and her breath escaped her in a deep sigh. She stayed there, against the wall, waiting as the lights went out inside the house. She'd give everyone time to get back into their rooms before she went in.

"Nancy!" the call was soft, a whisper. God, was she hearing things now? She didn't move and then it came again. "Nancy." She knew the voice, even whispered, and she turned. It was coming from the back corner of the house, by Cassie's herb garden. She moved through the darkness, carefully. "Here, Nancy ... over here," the whisper came. She turned to a dark patch of rhododendron alongside the corner of the house.

"Peter!" she gasped, her eyes focusing on the figure behind the bush. "You? They were chasing you?"

"Yes," he said, his voice strained. "Look, they'll have me if I stay here. They're working their way back in a circle."

"I know, I heard them," Nancy said.

"Can you get me into the house?" Peter asked. "They won't look there. If I can stay inside until they've closed the noose then I'll be able to leave. They'll quit then and go back to Wolf Hollow."

"The side door," Nancy said. "And then up to my room. You'll be safe there. I'll go in first. The others have gone back to bed, but Zachary might still be about. Watch the door. When you see me wave, come at once."

Peter nodded and Nancy turned and hurried back along the side of the house. She slipped into the side door, leaving it ajar. Inside, she paused and listened in the darkness. There was no sound. She waved an arm out of the door and a second later Peter was beside her. She led him up the stairs quickly and into the bolted safety of her room. He sat down on the edge of the bed. "Thanks," he said gratefully. I guess this makes us even in the favor department."

"Hardly," Nancy replied. "You're still at least two up on me. What were you doing, Peter? You told me never to go near Wolf Hollow and here you're inside it."

"It probably was pretty stupid of me but there was something I had to find out. It was the only way to do it."

"And did you find out what you wanted to find out?"

"No," he said angrily. "I was spotted too soon and the rest of the time I was busy running for my life."

"What were you trying to find, Peter?" Nancy asked. She saw his eyes, unsmiling, grave, fasten on her.

"I can't tell you," he said. "Not now, not until I know more. It's not something you even talk about, not without more facts than I have now. I could be doing a terrible injustice otherwise."

"Well, I've got something more," Nancy said. "That Seth Ordway, he has a huge purple strawberry mark on his hand."

"Yes, an hereditary thing with the Ordways, I've come to find out," Peter said. "It's quite common with them."

"The creature in the old house had one," Nancy said, searching Peter's eyes. "I'd completely forgotten about it until I saw the mark on Seth Ordway's hand."

She watched Peter get up and pace across the room. Finally he stopped and took her by the shoulders, looking gravely down at her. "I know what you're saying," he said. "That maybe there's a monstrous genetic aberration of the Ordways in Wolf Hollow which attacked you that night in the storm. But even if that did happen, it wouldn't mean a plot to kill you or that Jodie should have tried to do so. It would simply mean that you had a terrible experience that started and ended there."

"I guess it could just mean that," Nancy said slowly. "But there were signs on the old station, Peter, and signs on the roads, and there was that horror of a house."

"Still not necessarily so. All that still could have been the result of your experience that one night."

"You don't seem as certain about all this as you did, Peter," Nancy said. "Or are you just being gentler with me now?"

She saw Peter pause and consider for a moment, his eyes mirroring the care with which he struggled to choose his words.

"Not gentle, concerned," he answered. "I know what this business of the real and the unreal means to you. I don't want to do anything to destroy your belief in yourself. But I don't want to do anything to help you imagine the unreal as the real, either."

"You're a good person, Peter," Nancy said. "Good, kind, and understanding."

"It's not all that noble," he said. "It's pure self-interest."

His arms encircled her suddenly and his lips were on hers, warm, strong yet soft, and she pressed her body against his, aware of her nakedness under the shift. Finally he drew back and he was grinning down at her.

"You could be all wrong about me," he said. "You think I'm concerned over your mind and your emotional health. Maybe it's your body I'm really interested in getting to know better."

"You know, I don't really much care, so long as you're interested," Nancy answered boldly. She laid her head on his chest. "Oh, Peter, Peter, it's so wonderful feeling wanted again," she said. "I used to wonder if I could ever let myself feel wanted again. Or whether I would dare trust anyone ever again. But I'm not worried about that anymore."

"Good," was all Peter said. The sounds from outside made them break away from each other, and Nancy went to the window. The Ordways were moving in down the grassy slopes, closing the noose. The night mists had trailed away for the most part now, and she could see them converging in a loose circle. They halted just short of the house, and she saw others appearing from the sides. She could hear the disappointed murmurings of their voices and stayed to watch as they turned and walked off up over the ridge to finally disappear from sight.

Peter was suddenly at her side, and she looked up at his grave, serious face. "Did something for your work take you into Wolf Hollow?" she asked him.

"In a way," he said. "In a way." He kissed her hard, surprisingly hard. "Now you stay here and finish your work and keep out of trouble," he said. "No snooping around in the nights. I may have to go away for a day but I'll have Jed keep an eye on you."

"Will you tell me if you go?" Nancy asked, suddenly afraid.

"If I can," Peter said. "Now I've got to get out of here. It'll be dawn soon." He slipped from her arms and was gone in a second. She stayed by the window and watched his figure run from the side door across the grassy slope to the little path in the line of trees. She went to bed too tired to wonder about anything that night.

She slept late the next morning. When she went downstairs, Jodie was in the living room. She was wearing a brilliant orange blouse over white linen slacks. "You look especially gorgeous this morning," Nancy said. "That outfit didn't come from around here."

"I sent away for it from a catalogue," Jodie answered. Samuel Howell came into the room, and Nancy saw his eyes were cold, hard as flint as they speared her. He handed her the sketches for the kitchen. "Too much work to be done with these designs," he said brusquely. "Do me somethin' simple, somethin' a few coats of good paint can handle."

"All right, that shouldn't be difficult," Nancy said. The huge man was looking at her again with his eyes probing, small pinpoints in the folds of his face. Jodie, she saw, was being determinedly casual.

"You go outside last night by the side door, Miss Nancy?" Samuel Howell suddenly shot at her and Nancy almost jumped. She knew she hadn't been able to hide the surprise in her eyes and her mind raced.

"Why, yes," she said smoothly. "All that shooting and noise woke me and I couldn't go back to sleep. I thought I was being quiet about it. I'm sorry if I woke anyone."

"You didn't wake anyone," Jodie said.

"God," Nancy replied, feeling herself held by a deadly calmness. "I can't imagine then how you knew I'd gone out."

"There was some fresh dirt and leaves in the hallway by the door," Jodie said, a triumphant light in her eyes. Samuel Howell's eyes hadn't left Nancy's face, the girl knew. She could feel his piercing, probing look. Finally he grunted and turned and walked out. Nancy took her sketch pad and went into the kitchen. There she sat down alone on a high stool and felt the trembling inside her. Had she carried it off well enough? Had they believed her? She thought so but she couldn't be sure and suddenly there was an oppressive air of danger in this house. It was something she felt through her every pore, as though, for the first time, a mask had been ripped away. But what mask? She worked on simple designs using colors as the prime ingredient and had them finished by dinner time. The sense of danger hadn't disappeared, but work had made it possible to live with. At dinner, Samuel Howell was his usual expansive, charming self. Had his mood that morning been a result of something else and not really directed at her? He seemed to go out of his way to say as much.

"You know, Miss Nancy, I hope you didn't get the wrong impression earlier today," he said. "You are certainly free to go outside anytime of the day or night. I, and Jodie, too, had been concerned because of the marks we'd found in the side hall. Sometimes, because we are in a position of wealth around here, you might say, some folks think they can come a-stealin' and we don't take to that kindly."

"Naturally," Nancy said.

"Sometimes a nice walk in the night mists or under the moon is mighty good for settling a body down to sleep," he said. "So you feel free to do whatever you want to do around here."

"You're very kind," Nancy said and wondered if he were not almost urging her now to go out in the night. Perhaps he was being nothing but apologetic. Yet, she couldn't shake the feeling that games were being played here, deadly games that she could not understand. She went to her room after dinner, hurrying in, not even glancing down the dark hallway to the door at the end. A thought had been quietly gathering shape and force inside her, and now it burst forth. Bloodroots, the Howells, the Little Smokies, Deepwell Valley, the whole damned thing was more than she could cope with. The fears, the suspicions that had beset her, even if they were wrong, were too much to stand. The past was not dead long enough for her. She would leave, contract or no contract. It might be a mark against her if Samuel Howell complained to the school and the Association of Interior Designers, but her sanity was worth more than anything else. Tomorrow she would go to Peter and ask his advice, though she felt certain of what he'd say. It had started off all wrong that first night—that

still unexplained, hideous night that she would never forget—
and had gone downhill ever since. And perhaps it was more due
to her own sensitive imagination, she admitted. Yet it was beyond
her now and she would act on it.

Nancy turned off the light and undressed in the dark. The
night was less sultry than the one before, and the moon was
bright and high. Wearing only the tops of her pajamas, Nancy
went to the window, closed it a little and then, frowning, saw the
figure moving up toward the ridge. She saw the moon catch the
white slacks and even in the night, the brilliance of the orange
blouse gleamed as shafts of the cold blue light struck it. Nancy
watched as Jodie went to the ridge and began to slowly pace
back and forth on it, pausing now and then to lean against one
of the trees at the right side. Was the girl there watching to see
if she would leave the house again, Nancy asked herself. Nancy
watched for a while longer and then went to bed. But she called
on an inner alarm clock to wake her in a few hours. She slept, her
mind eased by her decision to leave this world within a world.
She woke later and got up, moving to the window. She rubbed
the sleep from her eyes and waited till her vision adjusted to the
night and the distance. Jodie was still there, on the ridge, and as
Nancy watched she saw the girl raise her arms upwards and move
in a kind of rhythm, a solitary dance under the moon. Nancy
watched until Jodie finished and went back to the darkness of
the trees. The girl was still there and half the night was gone.
She was clearly waiting and watching. Nancy went back and lay
down on the bed. She would tell Peter of this in the morning. He
would have to see the little pieces adding up. Jodie at the sluice
gates, her torn dress, Jodie waiting, watching for her to go out
in the night, perhaps hoping for another opportunity to kill her.
But why? Nancy threw aside the question. Any answers were so
far beyond reach as to be impossible. This was a valley of genetic
misfits and madness. Perhaps Jodie was one of them, despite her
lush, overwhelming, sensuous beauty.

Nancy finally went to sleep, and in the morning the sun was the only thing on the ridge. She had breakfast alone, just coffee which she made herself in the kitchen. She finished off a few last touches on the new drawings for the kitchen and left them where Samuel Howell would be sure to see them. Then she went outside, across the sunswept grass to the little path and down it to Peter's cabin. She had a grim kind of satisfaction in seeing that Jodie hadn't been up and about this morning. Her all-night vigil had undoubtedly taken its toll. The little cabin was silent as she emerged from the trail behind it. Not even Jed was lounging outside. The door was closed and, frowning, she knocked. Peter opened the door, a mug of tea in one hand, sleep still in his soft, hazel eyes, and wearing only trousers.

"Nancy," he exclaimed in surprise. "Come in. A social call?"

"Not completely," the girl said. "I think I've been more right than even I was willing to believe, Peter. Certainly about Jodie." She saw Peter frown and she quickly told him of how the Howells had first been upset that she should wander in the night and then switched attitudes completely. "And last night, Jodie waited on the ridge all night for me to go out again," Nancy said.

"Why did she wait?" Peter asked, frowning.

"For another chance to kill me," Nancy said. "Had I gone out, alone, in the night, she'd have managed to arrange something to make it look accidental. I only wish I knew if it were Jodie alone or if the others were involved. But she waited on the ridge last night, Peter. She waited there."

"How do you know it was Jodie?" he asked. "You've admitted those night mists play tricks. It could have been no one, or anyone."

"There were no mists last night, Peter, or hardly any, and the moon was bright," Nancy said. "It was Jodie. She had on that orange blouse and the white slacks she'd worn all day."

"It wasn't Jodie," Peter said quietly. "Jodie wasn't waiting on the ridge to follow you."

"But I saw her," Nancy said, anger rising inside her.

"It wasn't Jodie," he said stubbornly. "Just take my word for it."

"No, I won't take your word for it. I saw her," Nancy shot back. "How can you say it wasn't Jodie when you weren't even there?"

"Because Jodie spent the night here," he said quietly.

Nancy stood very still, letting his words sink deeply. What they meant about Jodie suddenly didn't seem that important. It was their other meaning that counted. She felt a little dizzy, light-headed, as though she'd been struck a blow that had left her swaying.

"I see," she finally managed through tight lips. "Thank you for telling me. It will help stop me from thinking the wrong thing about a lot of things." Peter reached out for her but she shrugged him away, stepped backwards.

"Nancy, you don't understand," he began.

"Oh, but I do," she said. "I'm just not interested in stepping into Jodie's place after you leave here, until whoever might be next comes along."

"You've got it all wrong," Peter said. "You're jumping to conclusions again."

"And they've been pretty right so far," Nancy snapped.

"I was trying to find out something and I thought that way, with Jodie, might help me find out," Peter said.

"And most enjoyably, I'm sure," Nancy sniffed. "Good-bye, Peter."

She turned and ran onto the road, glad that Peter didn't try to chase after her. She didn't want him seeing how far she had let her hopes and desires carry her. She didn't want him seeing how naïvely foolish she had been. It was her own fault, clutching at his kindness, reading too, too much into his kisses, seeing things she wanted to see in his soft eyes. She seemed to have a failing for that sort of thing, she reminded herself bitterly. And last night, as she thought of Peter's concern for her, he was spending the night enjoying Jodie's raw, sensuous body. Tears misted her eyes as she hurried up the road. Being wrong seemed a built-in part of her insofar as men were concerned. And about how much else, she had to wonder again. The figure she'd seen on the ridge last night had been Cassie, of course, acting out more of her own sick games in Jodie's clothes. Had that shattered her conclusions about Jodie? Had she any right to cling to them now? Strangely enough, despite everything, her suspicions persisted. More and more she was becoming convinced that there had to be a key, an answer to all that had happened. Even the strange madness of this land had to have an explanation of some sort.

She had gone more than halfway toward the big house, her mind racing, consumed with its own turbulent thoughts, when a woman stepped out from behind a tree to block her path.

"Miss Hazelton, I've got to talk to you," the woman said. Nancy halted, staring at the women before her. She was small, thin, dressed neatly in a print dress, somehow different from anyone she'd seen here in this valley of blood and feuds and madness. "I've been trying to get to you but you've always been with someone or they've been watching me too closely."

"Who are you?" Nancy asked. "What do you want with me?"

The woman glanced around nervously, fear in her eyes. "I can't explain much," she said. "Someone may come and see me here with you and everything would be finished. You don't know me, of course. I live in Deepwell Junction. But it's my husband. He's got to talk to you."

Nancy frowned. The woman's fear was no act, she saw. Her eyes kept darting up and down the road, searching the trees.

"I've only been able to sneak away a few times without being seen," the woman said, wringing her hands nervously. Nancy saw that perspiration was staining the simple print she wore. "They can't see me up here. I must get back home."

"*They?*" Nancy echoed. "Who are *they?*"

"The Ordways," the woman said. "They keep watch constantly. There's danger, terrible danger, for you, for my husband. Please, you must go to him, tonight. You must do as he says."

"Why can't he come to the house to see me?"

"He's in hiding. He's been there ever since that night. If you value your life, you'll go and see him. Do you know where Rock Lake is?"

Nancy nodded. "Go past it, along the side of the rocks that go up to the main lake. You'll find a big old oak, split in two by lightning. Take the trail next to it, into the rocks. There's a cave. He's there."

"Look, I don't know about all this," Nancy began. "I don't think I can promise anything like that."

"Please, or you're dead, both of you," the woman said. "Please go to him. I can't say more. I don't know anymore, really."

The woman turned and faded into the trees. Nancy heard her moving away through the woods, moving quickly. The girl waited and then walked on, slowly now, going over the woman's words in her mind. When she reached the house, Samuel Howell was on the porch, arguing with Jodie. Their angry voices could be heard almost at the start of the broad expanse of the beautiful star-pointed flowers with the name so appropriate to this land. They broke off their arguing as Nancy came into view, and Jodie disappeared inside the house. Samuel Howell's small pinpoint eyes followed Nancy as the girl went upstairs without speaking. Somehow, it seemed time to stop playing games all around.

# CHAPTER EIGHT

Nancy sat in her room and watched the night descend on the hills, the hollows, the ridge, turning each one from a cool, sylvan spot into a place of mystery and slowly rising mist. All afternoon she had turned the woman's words over in her mind. All afternoon she had reviewed everything that had happened to her since she came here that first, storm-shattered night. Or, being meticulously honest with herself, everything she believed had happened to her. And it all wound itself into an ever-tightening knot of unexplained, unfathomable mystery, without rhyme or reason, either for happening or even for being imagined. The real and the unreal once again, slipping and sliding into each other, separating, seeming to stand out suddenly, only to fade away into each other's shadows. Even Peter was a part of it. She'd thought his concern for her to be the most important thing to him, his eyes holding a reality for her. And that, too, had been less than real, more of her own wishful thinking than anything else.

Then now, suddenly, this frightened little woman with talk of terrible danger and people hiding in caves. It could all have been merely a clever device to send her into the night, to her death. And yet, somehow, this woman's talk had had more reality in it than anything else in this lush valley. There was the reality of fear in it. She'd felt it, unmistakably. She was, if nothing else she said grimly to herself, an authority on the realness of fear, the look of it, the smell of it, the feel of it. And this little woman had been afraid. So, as the hours went on and the night deepened, Nancy decided to follow the little woman's plea. The heart, not the head, had been the wisest when all was said and done. Her heart had misled her into loving Dirk, but it had tried to warn her finally. Only she'd refused to listen. She'd listen now.

Nancy changed into slacks and a deep blue blouse, dark colors for the dark of the night. She went softly down the hall, down the stairway, and out the side door. It was nearly midnight, and the mists were painting the ridge and the hollow with their gray brush. She hurried through them, up over the ridge on the same path she'd taken to Rock Lake. Over the ridge the mists continued to shroud her hurrying figure, but when she reached the narrow trail by the birches they fell back and she climbed into clear night air. The moonlight cast its cold light on the rocks and sparkled through the trees on the waters of the little lake. She went on, past the lake, as the woman had said. The big oak tree was impossible to miss, split down the center and leaning in opposite directions, a giant, gnarled V in the moonlight. She found the trail alongside it, turning sharply and going into the heavy rocks. She climbed, her throat dry, becoming more apprehensive as she went. Yet somehow she did not feel fear, not real fear. The boulders cast black circles of darkness in the moonlight, and she used their smooth sides to clamber up the rocky path. She paused as she saw a small opening in one cluster of rocks, a cave. Then she went on, loose pebbles clattering loudly down the trail as her foot dislodged them. She'd gone some ten yards further when she heard a man's voice and saw the larger opening in the rock.

"In here," the voice said. "It's all right." Nancy stayed on the path, peering into the blackness. A figure came out, unshaven, bearded, yet there was something recognizable about him, a nervous, fluttery way in which he moved his hands. Suddenly she gasped.

"You're the conductor on the train!" she exclaimed.

"Yes," the man said. "That's right. I'm glad my wife finally contacted you. Please come in."

Nancy followed the man into the cave and saw, around a corner of it, a small fire, not more than glowing coals. But it gave some light and some warmth. He sat down beside it, and Nancy sank to her knees. Her mind was racing with a torrent of thoughts trying to fall into place, pushing and jostling each other in her head, leaping up to shout out with disconnected insistence.

"Then you did put me off at the old abandoned station, didn't you?" Nancy leaped forward in thought.

"Yes, the old station," the man said. Nancy felt the sweet triumph of right but she forced herself to slow her racing thoughts.

"Suppose you start from the beginning," she said. "Tell me what this is all about."

"I can't tell you that, ma'm," the man said, his voice still high, wavery, nervous. "I can only tell you what I know. Sam Howell told Tom and me to take the train onto the old spur line and let you off at the old station. He promised Tom and me a right nice piece of change."

"Who is Tom?" Nancy interrupted.

"Tom Featherwell, the engineer," the man said. "Tom and me, we pretty much run the little old train line that goes through the Smokies proper. Well, as I say, Sam Howell promised us real nice money. He had us put up the old signs on the station and on the roads a few days before. All we had to do then was to switch onto the old track and let you off at the old station. Then we circled around to rejoin the new track down the way apiece."

"But why?" Nancy asked. The conductor shrugged, rubbing his unshaven face with one hand.

"I don't know that, ma'am," he said. "But I do know that when Tom went to collect the next night he never did come back. He ain't never been seen since, either, I hear."

Nancy saw a figure running on the ridge as her mind flashed back, and blood in the bushes and a railroad engineer's cap still in the closet of her room at the Manor house.

"I know what that meant," the man was going on. "I've lived around here long enough for that. I went into hiding, up here. My wife manages to sneak out to bring me some food but they're watching her like hawks, waiting for me to show up or her to lead them to me. I told her to try and get to you. You've got to get away from here and tell somebody somethin'. That or I'll get caught sooner or later."

"But it doesn't make any sense at all," Nancy exclaimed. "What do you know about an old house in Wolf Hollow and a sub-human creature that lives around there?"

"Not a thing, ma'm, not a thing," the little man answered. "All I know is what I've told you. Maybe you can fit the rest together. But I know something bad's going on, somethin' real bad."

Nancy stared into the glowing embers of the little fire. She had been right all along. There had been the abandoned old station and the signs. It had all been arranged so she would start walking and find her way to the derelict of a house. It had been planned from the very beginning, perhaps even from the phone call that had brought her here in the first place. But the one word continued to leap out, larger and larger each time. Why? Why, why, why? She had kneeled by a window sill and called that out once before. But it was too late then for an answer. This time she would find the answer. She couldn't leave here without it, she knew, not and ever be sane again. And perhaps she would never leave alive anyway. But she would die knowing the answer to that one question, she promised herself. Why? She would learn that answer before anything else.

Nancy got to her feet, a grimness on her like a cloak. "Get out of Deepwell Valley, get help someplace," the little man said. "I'll stay here as long as I can."

"I'll do my best," Nancy said. She turned and walked from the cave, making her way down the rocky path, past the huge split oak and the sparkling water of the little lake. One fact hammered inside her head as she walked. It had been planned. Someone wanted her killed. It was inconceivable. There wasn't a reason she could even conjure up. And yet it was true. And perhaps there was no reason, at least not the rational kind she wanted. Madness needs no reason, she knew. Madness is its own reason and surely they were all mad here in this backwater of the world. Samuel Howell had promised money to arrange her death that first night. Had he known the sub-human creature would see her move toward the old house? He must have, Nancy told herself. She would simply have vanished, and if her body was ever found, the passage of time would have erased all signs of what had really happened.

And now, with sickening clarity, the argument between Jodie and her father made sense. They had argued over who was to kill her. Jodie wanted the pleasure, too, it seemed. She'd tried it on her own and roused the elder Howell's fury. But again why, she cried inside herself, an anguished, bitter cry. A few short weeks ago she had never heard of these people or this land. The unreasoning monstrousness of it made her stomach turn over. She was walking through the night mists once again, up over the ridge and down toward the house. She slowed her angry pace and crept along the dark line of the trees until she was opposite the house. Then, vanishing into a heavy layer of mist that rolled past, she crossed to the house and went in by the side door. The house was silent and she tip-toed up to her room, sliding the bolt on as soon as she'd closed the door.

Nancy sank down on the bed and suddenly felt the weakness of her legs, the trembling of her body as finally she reached to what she had learned this night. She lay there and thought again of that one burning question. But more and more she was coming to wonder if the answer, somehow, wasn't tied up with the deserted horror of a house in Wolf Hollow. There had to be some reason why it had all been arranged for her to find her way to it. There must be at least some symbolic reason behind it, perhaps both a practical and a symbolic one. Before her mind faltered from sheer exhaustion she promised herself to go to see Peter in the morning. He would have to believe, now. Finally, she fell asleep, drained of thought and action for the night.

# CHAPTER NINE

JODIE, CASSIE, AND SAMUEL HOWELL were breakfasting in the dining room when Nancy went downstairs in the morning. She forced herself to have coffee with them and listen to the huge man's florid, folded face approve her designs. She made herself think of how she used to force herself to listen to the doctors and nurses at the sanatorium, playing along with their little games. Only then the roles had been reversed. Now the mad ones were across the table from her, Jodie with her lush, sensuous body. It was odd, she recalled, how she had sensed the decay in that over-ripe body the first time she'd seen it. Almost mischievously, she silently wondered what Peter would think of his recent bedmate when he heard the truth about her. And Cassie, angular stepchild of beauty, living her thrills by the stories Jodie obviously told her of lovemaking. And Samuel Howell, most normal appearing and perhaps maddest of them all. Yet she was sitting here, the intended victim with the executioners. But they were executioners who had failed, each of them once, except for Cassie. They would fail again. She smiled sweetly, excused herself, and went outside, crossing quickly to the little shortcut to Peter's cabin.

Jed, lounging outside, made her heart leap in warmth. But his eyes were narrowed, looking closely at her as she reached the cabin. The door was closed and Jed spoke to her in his cadenced rhythm.

"Mister Peter's not there," Jed said. "He went off, suddenly."

"Went off?" Nancy frowned, her heart sinking. "Went off where? For how long?"

"He didn't tell me," Jed said. "He went off last night. He said he didn't want anyone to even know he was gone and that if any-one asked, to say he'd gone into town. All except you. He said I could tell you the truth if you came askin'."

Nancy's heart was lead. Peter could be gone days. She could be dead when he returned. Time was running out, she somehow knew inside her. She'd finished her designs and Samuel Howell knew she had finished them in a hurry. He had to have sensed that she felt something was wrong. Tonight, she told herself, she would flee tonight. She'd just keep going until she got out of this valley of madness. But not before she'd learned why Samuel Howell had gone to such elaborate lengths to kill her, why he had reached out to pluck her from the city and bring her here to slay her. And she still felt certain that the answer lay in the old house. Perhaps it would be only a scrap of something. Perhaps only a faded picture. Or perhaps there would be nothing. That would be an answer of its own. It would tell her that fate had marked her for this strange experience, or perhaps for death, just as fate had marked her mother for death and her grandmother to die in childbirth.

She looked up to see Jed studying her. She took his arm and probed those bland, expressionless eyes. "I want you to help me, Jed," she said. "Do you know a secret way to get into Wolf Hollow, a way that's not far from the old station?"

She saw Jed withdraw, start to shake his head.

"It's very important to me, Jed," she said. "Maybe the most important thing ever to me. I'm sure you know a way. You know every path and trail in this valley, Jed. Please, do this for me."

She saw the struggle behind his eyes, an uncertainty of which course to take. "Tonight, Jed, come to Bloodroots," she said. "I'll have a letter for you for Peter. You can tell me then."

Jed nodded and she squeezed his arm, then turned and hur-ried back up the little trail. Peter's car was gone, she noted, and it made her more certain that she couldn't risk waiting for him to return. She would act tonight, once and for all.

There was a strange calmness upon her the rest of the day. Jodie wasn't about and Samuel Howell apparently was keeping to his room. Only Cassie showed herself, working in her herb garden. The calmness would, she knew, disappear soon enough, but while it lasted she enjoyed it and it let her think back quietly on the past. More and more she was coming to wonder about the workings of the thing called fate, destiny, kismet. Once she would have scoffed at dark stars, at events beyond the control of man. But now she scoffed at nothing. It even seemed appropriate that she should have known where the kitchen was here in Bloodroots Manor, and where the cellar steps went down. At least it was no more unreal than anything else that had happened here. And once again she had been right all along. The unreal had been real. Impatiently Nancy waited for the night to come. Where had Peter gone, she wondered. And why so suddenly, so secretively? Even with Peter there were strange things that begged the question *why?* As the shadows grew longer and she saw the sun vanish, she sat down at the table, took a piece of paper from her sketch pad, and folded it down to note size. Stationery was something she hadn't brought along. With her hand surprisingly steady, she began to write.

Dear Peter,

I will be gone when you read this. Tonight I am going to find that old house once again, the last piece in this mad, mad puzzle. I have learned that everything I told you was true. Samuel Howell arranged everything to kill me. But I don't know why. Unless I find this out, I will never be sane, really sane. I couldn't live a life with another unanswered why. If I am destined to be pursued by madmen, I want to know that much at least.

When I leave here I will run, as fast and far as I can. If I am not at my apartment in a day, you will know I have never left Deepwell Valley. Contact the wife of the railroad conductor in Deepwell Junction then. I'm truly sorry you weren't here.

Nancy.

Nancy fashioned a crude envelope for the letter from a piece of sketch pad paper, sealing it with a small tube of rubber cement she had as part of her work materials. It was dark now, and she went downstairs and out the side door. She waited in the shadows, her eyes scanning the grassy slope, looking for Jed's slender figure. But he found her, calling to her softly from a cluster of bushes beyond the house. She went to him and saw the little frown on his smooth brow, contrasting strangely with the elfin smile that still played on his face.

"I don't know that I'm doing right," he said.

"You're doing what I want you to do, Jed," Nancy said, a little ashamed for using her charms on him. She handed him the letter. "This is for Peter," she said. "Please give it to him as soon as he gets back."

Jed nodded, taking the letter in his hand. "How do I get into Wolf Hollow, Jed?" Nancy asked softly. Jed answered, not raising his eyes, looking at the ground.

"A way near the old station, you said," he murmured. "Take the ridge down, right along it, and you'll reach the old station. Go to the right then, to a pin cherry. You'll see the berries on it. Go in there. The trail is right behind it. It winds between a small rocky ravine."

"Thank you, Jed," Nancy said. "I'll wait till later, when I'm certain everyone's asleep." Jed faded away into the mists that began to rise, and Nancy returned to her room. She waited patiently, looking out the window to see if Cassie were wandering about. But the night was still, and finally she went down and out the side door again. The girl walked quickly through the night, moving with the mists. At the ridge, she turned and followed the line of it as it descended steadily. It was a long descent with some straight sections and then down again deeper into the valley. Finally she saw the dark bulk of the station loom up at the bottom of the path, the moon striking the slanted roof. As she reached the station, the moon suddenly disappeared and she looked up to see the fast-moving, dark clouds blotting out the silver sphere. In the distance, the rumble of thunder sounded. How appropriate, Nancy said to herself grimly. Hurrying she went down the road, her eyes searching the wall of trees until she saw the pin cherry, the small red fruits on the slender twigs with the narrow leaves. She ducked into the forest behind the tree and almost immediately found herself on the narrow path between two sides of rock about four feet in height.

The earlier calmness deserted her, and she heard the harshness of her breathing and felt the dryness in her throat. The thunder rumbled again, a little louder this time, and it hurried her footsteps. The rocks suddenly came to an end and she was in the woods, the hanging branches once again clutching at her, and she was trembling, her mind a motion picture projector going backwards, flashing images in front of her. She saw the figure running on the ridge, pursued by something, and she regretted not having found out what was behind the closed door at the end of the corridor. Cascading water flashed in front of her eyes, and her figure being swept onto the rocks, and then she saw a hideous creature chasing her, slashing at her with long arms. The projector switched off abruptly and only the stygian silence greeted her. She moved forward and a dark bulk loomed in front of her through the trees. She rushed forward, stumbling, catching herself on a branch and half-falling into the little clearing. There was no lightning this time, but the derelict of a house still stood there, a toothless crone that she'd remembered, a place for cauldrons and witches and the stink of death. She moved forward into it, up the rotted front steps and through the splintered door lying on the floor. The big room was just as she'd remembered it, the fireplace at the far end. She would need more light to examine it more closely, she knew and, as she'd done that first night, she lighted a fire with the dried old wood in the fireplace. The flames crackled quickly, and in moments the room was lighted by the dancing, flickering fire.

Nancy glanced around at the walls, seeking some old picture perhaps, some clue to this place. A dust-covered bureau stood against one wall, down at one end because of its broken legs. She pulled open the drawers, looking into each one. But they were all empty.

"You won't find anythin'," the voice said, and Nancy spun around to see the full, sensuous figure in the doorway.

"Jodie!" Nancy gasped and, as the girl moved into the room, she saw the firelight glint from the huge blade of the kitchen knife she held in one hand. Jodie's deep, liquid eyes had become black lights, just as she'd seen eyes like hers do once before. "How did you know I was here?" Nancy said, watching the other girl advance.

"Your friend Jed Batterbee," Jodie said. "Zachary caught him as he went away after meeting you. Daddy took the letter from him."

Nancy heard the sound of her own breath as it drew in sharply. "Why, Jodie?" she asked the girl. "Why? What did I ever do to you? Why me?"

"Dirk is dead because of you," Jodie said simply.

"Dirk?" Nancy gasped again. She felt her mind staggered by the unexpectedness of the name. "What do you know about Dirk?"

"Dirk was very close to me," Jodie said. "Close to all of us."

Nancy watched the black brown liquid depths of Jodie's eyes, twin pools of unfathomable blackness, and suddenly her skin began to crawl, her chest grow tight with icy bands. It was plain now, so very plain, and she'd seen it before, the eyes, the defiant lift of the chin, the sensuous beauty. She'd seen it but she hadn't made the connection, of course.

"He was your brother," Nancy heard herself say, her voice hardly able to speak the words.

Jodie moved quickly, catlike, and Nancy found herself forced back against the broken bureau, the point of the knife against her left breast. Despite it, she heard her voice again, echoing her own words in shocked disbelief. "He was your brother," she rasped.

"He was beautiful, wasn't he?" Jodie said, her eyes burning coals of black fire. "He wrote me about you. He told me how he was driving you mad. His body was beautiful to lay next to, wasn't it? He was wonderful to touch, wasn't he?"

The knife point moved against her breast, drawing blood. "Wasn't he?" Jodie screamed suddenly.

"Yes, yes," Nancy answered. Jodie drew the knife back a fraction.

"But he never held you, not really," Jodie sneered. "You never felt his body hard against yours, smooth and strong, the feel of him on you."

"You were in love with him?" Nancy heard herself whisper incredulously. "You loved him, not as a brother, as a lover."

"You never had him as either," Jodie snarled and Nancy felt herself flinch. Even now the truth hurt, the bitter words struck deep. Even now.

"And you killed him," Jodie said, her voice ice.

"It was an accident. I didn't mean for it to happen. He was trying to kill me, to push me out the window."

Nancy saw the girl draw her hand back for an instant, getting room to lunge forward with the knife. She twisted away and felt the steel slash across her shoulder. But she was away from the bureau now and circling as Jodie advanced slowly.

"Dirk tried to kill me," Nancy said. "Why?"

"He's dead because of it, because of you," Jodie said. "That's why it's for me to kill you. I told Pa I would and I'm goin' to do it now." Jodie moved forward, lashed out in arc with the knife and Nancy stumbled backwards, just preventing herself from falling.

But it was clear that Jodie knew how to use the knife, and it was only a matter of time before the blade would sink into Nancy's flesh. "Why, Jodie, why?" Nancy half-cried. She had to know that much at least. But the girl only moved forward, catlike, closing in on her prey. Nancy saw that she was being maneuvered into a corner and she tried to move to the left. The blade sliced the air and she fell back. The corner was but a scant six inches behind her now. Once there it would be the end for her. She tried another dash, this time to the right. Jodie went with her, quick as a cat, and the knife just grazed her arm. Jodie was grinning now, a grimace of triumph, the same, the very same coldly triumphant smile she had seen once before as Dirk rushed toward the window.

The half-roar, half-snarl burst into the room. Jodie spun around and Nancy, looking past her, saw the creature in the doorway. No memory could make it more hideous than it was, the mouth working feverishly, opening and closing as it gulped air, the wild whites of its eyes flashing. Nancy, with Jodie's attention momentarily distracted, ducked under the knife and raced across the room.

"No, no, damn no," she heard Jodie scream. The creature leaped forward toward the two girls. Nancy glanced back to see Jodie rushing after her, the knife upraised. "It's my right," the girl was screaming. "It's mine." A piece of wood on the floor tripped Nancy. She felt herself go down, turning to look at Jodie again as she did. She saw the creature reach out its long, swinging arms and Jodie duck away from its grasp. Nancy regained her feet, moved sideways toward the door. The creature turned to her, moved to cut her off, small bubbling sounds coming from it. It leaped forward for her and Nancy felt herself freeze. "No!" she heard Jodie's scream. "Mine, mine!"

The girl darted forward to plunge the knife into Nancy. The creature's arms, sweeping out, caught her. Nancy fell back against the wall and saw the creature's hands tear the blouse from Jodie's overflowing breasts, nails like claws digging into her.

Jodie screamed and the creature flung her to the ground and was atop her at once, ripping at her, covering her with its blubbering, gaping mouth. Jodie's screams were muffled but they still cut through the night with agonizing terror. Nancy turned and ran toward the door, when the huge figure in the white suit appeared in the doorway. She darted to one side as Samuel Howell came into the room, his massive head dark with anger, his eyes finding the struggling figures on the floor. Jodie's screams had ceased, and Samuel Howell rushed forward.

"Damn you, girl," he shouted. "Damn, I told you to leave it to me!" Then Nancy saw him raise his arm, saw the heavy revolver in his hand. He fired, pumping one, two, three, four bullets into the creature. As the shots exploded in the old house, Nancy ran out the door and into the woods, racing headlong through the branches, falling over bushes, scraping her legs on thorns and sharp twigs as she had done that first night. She heard the sound of someone running after her and then the shot and the whine of the bullet as it slammed into the trees. She dodged, ran to the right, hoping her sense of direction would hold up. Behind her, the white linen suit of Samuel Howell could be glimpsed, the big man pushing his way through the brush with the inexorableness of a tank. Then she heard voices, other voices, and Samuel Howell's booming answers. The Ordways, she knew, his guardians of Wolf Hollow, entrusted with the task of keeping prying eyes from the presence of the decaying old house in its midsts. There were so many things yet unanswered. In fact, the one staggering answer she had learned only opened up a Pandora's box of other questions.

"Spread out," she heard Samuel Howell thunder, and she was suddenly grateful for the blackness of the deep woods. She dropped to the ground and began to crawl, moving her body along the ground, fighting down the sharp pain of rocks and thorns that pressed into her breasts, her stomach, her legs. She heard the sound of her pursuers moving through the woods on both sides, searching for her, and she even managed a grim smile as she heard them finally turn off and strike out to the right and left. But she continued to crawl, painfully slowly but hidden by the underbrush. Then, when the sounds of their footsteps had faded away completely, she rose to her feet and rushed on. The single shot snapped a branch just over her head and she ducked to glance back. Samuel Howell's white suit stood out in the darkness. He had not gone off with the others but continued to move slowly forward, silent for all his bulk. Nancy ran, dodging from right to left, and suddenly the ground was sloping down sharply and memory gave her feet renewed speed. Samuel Howell was running after her now, the sound of his huge bulk crashing through the trees, obviously realizing she was nearing the end of the woods.

A sudden steep decline sent Nancy crashing into branches and logs, and once more memory flew to her. She had fallen here that first night, too. She got up and ran, the trees suddenly opening up onto the dirt road. Her feet flew down the road. Peter's cabin, she gasped. It had to be near here someplace. Suddenly lights appeared ahead of her, the twin headlights of a car coming up the road. She ran out in front of it, waving frantically. The lights struck her figure, blinding her for the moment, bathing her in their glare and then she saw the tall, sandy-haired man racing toward her, pulling her to the car.

"Peter," she gasped out. "Oh, God, Peter!"

"You little fool," he said angrily but his eyes were deep with concern. "Why didn't you wait until I came back?"

He was pushing her into the car and she saw Jed there, a deep gash on the side of his temple. "I got away from them after they caught me," he explained. "I came here and waited for Mister Pete."

The shot whistled over the open top of the car. "Get down," Peter yelled, and Nancy saw him flick off the headlights as he dived out of the car. She saw his body roll off the side of the road, into the darkness of the bushes there, and then, peering through the windshield, she saw Samuel Howell moving down the road toward them. He was moving fast and he fired again. The shot ripped into the top of the back seat and Nancy huddled down half atop of Jed. He would be on them in moments, pumping bullets into their huddled forms. She could hear the sound of his footsteps. Then there was another sound, and she looked up in time to see Peter lunging from the side in a flying tackle, catching the huge man around the knees. She saw Samuel Howell go down, sideways like a building toppling, and then Peter was on top of him, grappling for the gun. The big man used his weight to roll over, tossing Peter from his grip. A shot ran out, but she saw Peter get his head down in time and once again grab Samuel Howell's gun hand, forcing it backwards. The huge man got to one knee and flung himself forward, carrying Peter with him. But this time Peter held his grip, clinging like a wildcat on a hound's back. Now Nancy saw the silent figures that had come to the edge of the trees and were watching, too. But no one took action, sensing this was a battle of finality, a decision that encompassed more than they could imagine.

Samuel Howell slipped, carrying Peter with him, and she could hear the big man's breath was rasping, almost gone. Nancy felt her hands tighten, her nails digging into her palms, as Samuel Howell brought his arm up and around, forcing Peter's hand back. The gun moved up, aiming at Peter's chest, and then Peter rolled away, still clinging to his grip, pulling the big man with him. They rolled over in the dirt and Nancy couldn't get a clear view. A shot—the sound of final judgement—followed by absolute silence. Watching, her hands trembling, Nancy saw Samuel Howell's huge form finally go limp, saw his hand with the gun still in it, fall to his side. Peter got up slowly, twisting his neck, stretching his shoulder muscles, and walked to the car. Nancy saw the Ordways fade into the trees like so many dark wraiths.

Peter climbed into the car, turned it, and drove back to the cabin. Only when they were inside the warmth of its light did Nancy speak.

"Dirk was Jodie's brother," she said quietly. "He was a Howell. They're mad, all of them mad."

"Yes, but not quite the way you mean it," Peter said. "Dirk's attempt to kill you was planned. His meeting you, making you fall in love with him, it was all planned."

"Why, in God's name? Why, Peter?" Nancy rasped.

"It took me a while to put it together," Peter said. "And when I first began to suspect the truth, the enormity of it was more than I could make myself believe. It even meant that all that happened to you over the past year was in a way because of me."

Nancy looked up at the tall, lean man, frowning in confusion, and he put a hand on her shoulder. "Little things stuck in my mind, even though I dismissed them at first. When I took you to the old station that day, for example. I found some oil spots on the rusted old tracks. But I told myself that it was entirely possible an engine could have pushed some cars onto the spur line for a few hours. And all the things you told me stuck with me, despite the plausible reasons I gave you and myself. But it was the song that Jed sang for me that pulled it all together suddenly."

"The song?" Nancy echoed.

"Yes, the song. I told you that the origins and history of these people is reflected in the music and words of their folk songs, the ballads and reels and narrative songs. Remember I told you of a family named Cragshead who seemed to have up and disappeared?"

Nancy nodded and Peter gestured to Jed. She saw Jed pick up his guitar, turn toward her and begin to sing.

*"Now listen here friends and I'll tell you a story,*
*'Bout the night the Howells went down in their glory,*

*Of an evil that lies down in the ground,*
*Of a secret that's buried and bound.*

*There'd been feudin' and fightin' between them so,*
*The Howells and Cragsheads, the high and the low,*
*And no one lives now who was there that night,*
*But for many a year they sang of that fight.*

*The Cragsheads came stealin' through the dark, dark still,*
*Ready and eager and waitin' to kill,*
*The Howells were sleeping but they woke up to fight,*
*And the sound of the killing shattered the night.*

*'Tis said that for days the valley ran red,*
*And old man Howell was killed in his bed.*
*And when it was over, my friends, believe me,*
*It was the end of the Howells and all their family,*
*Wiped out by the Cragsheads on a dark night in June,*
*With no one to see, not even the moon."*

Jed put down the guitar and Nancy looked up at Peter, her face dark with disbelief. "The end of the Howells?" she said. "But that song's got it all wrong. It must have been the end of the Cragsheads."

"That's what I said when I heard it," Peter replied. "I had Jed sing it ten times for me, and he swore up and down that the song was accurate to the last word, just as it had been handed down for generations. I trust Jed on these things. I've learned his songs are history and he was adamant on this one. It bugged me and I went to my records. I found out when it was that the Cragsheads seemed to have just up and disappeared. From the time Jed dates that song, it was the exact same time."

"But that proves what I just said," Nancy answered. If the Cragsheads just disappeared it was because the Howells killed them in that fight the song tells about."

"Only if the song is wrong," Peter said slowly. "I began to think about what it meant if the song was right and the pieces I found later began to fit in perfectly. I learned, for example, that story has it that there was a woman, a Howell, who was pregnant at the time of the fight in the song. She ran away to Louisville and died in childbirth."

Nancy felt her breath drain away. "You mean my grandmother?" she asked. "My mother's mother?"

"I checked out the birth records in Louisville going way back," Peter said. "There was a woman by the name of Howell who died in childbirth. You see, the song tells only part of what happened, a thing we call the ugly name of fratricide."

"But if the song is right, who are these Howells?"

"Descendents of the Cragsheads," Peter said. "When the Cragsheads wiped out the Howells way back then, they not only took over the Howell's home, Bloodroots, and their possessions, but their identity. They became the Howells. They got themselves a new identity, a ruling position, and the income from the outside properties the original Ezra Howell had developed. In this isolated community, ruled by power and blood feuds, where no one spoke to outsiders and outsiders didn't enter, it was really quite a simple transformation. And as time went by, those who knew the truth died off, and the descendants of those original Cragsheads just carried on as Howells.

"And Dirk and I, where does that all fit in?"

"Because the past wasn't dead yet," Peter said. "You see, the Cragsheads knew the lie they lived and though they were relatively secure, there were one or two danger spots. They knew your grandmother had given birth to a girl that had been taken east and raised, and they kept watch on that girl as she grew. It seemed that she'd pose them no problem but then, as I got into this thing deeper, I found that a funny thing happened. I also recalled how you said your mother had been killed in a freak accident twenty-five years or so ago. I looked up some county records and found that the state had sent a man into Deepwell Valley twenty-five years ago to do pretty much what I've done, trace a pattern of family history and take a census. He never got far it seemed and soon quit, but his presence was enough to trigger the Cragsheads into action. If he had somehow gotten hold of old records or stirred up enough dust, he might have found holes in spots. He might even have traced your mother down and asked questions. The Cragsheads knew that their whole house of cards could be brought down around their heads. But not if your mother, and you, the only living links with the real Howells, were dead. Any investigation would come to an end right at that spot."

"So the accident wasn't an accident but planned murder," Nancy said.

"Exactly," Peter went on. "But because of you and your sudden attack of measles, they were only half successful. You still lived. However, when the investigator gave up and quit, things settled down again."

"Until you showed up last year," Nancy said. "Then the same possibility rose again."

"That's right," Peter said. "And I was doing a much more thorough job of snooping around. You were the one living link left that might, if traced, do them in. An investigation might even have set you up to tracing back on your own and causing trouble that way, too."

"So they sent Dirk to find me, to make me fall in love with him, to marry me, and then kill me."

"Making it seem like an accident, of course," Peter said. "With you dead, they would have no more worries ever. But when that failed at the last moment, Samuel Howell devised his scheme to bring you down here."

An emptiness was upon Nancy, a terrible, depressing emptiness. The *why* had been answered, finally, and for that she could be grateful. But the enormous sickness of it all made her feel drained, emptied of even pity.

"When I went to Louisville yesterday and then called a friend back east to have him check the date of that accident to your mother and father, and found it coincided with the time the investigator was here, I knew that was the final piece to prove it all," Peter said. "Of course, had it all worked out as he'd planned it that first night, the creature would have killed you and Samuel Howell Cragshead would have had his way. You were lucky that night, too, Nancy."

Nancy leaned her head against Peter. "I was lucky when you found me," she said softly. "That's when my luck started. What was that horrible thing, anyway? It was sub-human, Peter."

"No doubt," Peter said. "I'd guess it was one of the Ordways, some genetic mutation, the result of generations of inbreeding. Obviously Samuel Howell kept it at the manor, probably trained like some dog, to kill on being let loose."

Nancy shuddered. She knew now she'd been practically living next door to it all the while. She was glad she hadn't ever decided to open that door at the end of the hallway.

"Backing the Ordways in their absolute control of Wolf Hollow kept anyone from seeing the old house where the original Cragsheads once lived," Peter said. "Some strange sentimentality apparently kept every generation of Cragsheads from burning it down."

"Why did I know where the kitchen was at Bloodroots?" Nancy asked, her hand finding Peter's, holding tightly to his. "And the cellar steps, why did I know about them?"

"Now you're in an area of psychic phenomena no one can really explain, Nancy," he said. "We don't know that much about the mind, about the inherited powers of memory, of the psyche itself. The more we investigate, the more we learn how little we know. From somewhere in the past, you had a flash of psychic knowledge. Of course, you didn't, you couldn't connect it with a past you'd never been aware of."

"But now it's over, Peter," Nancy said, pressing her head against Peter.

"Yes, it's over now," he said. She heard a movement and turned to see Jed disappearing out the door. She started to call out to him but Peter put a finger to her lips, gently.

"Tomorrow," he said. He lifted her to her feet and then his lips were on hers, pressing her mouth open, kissing her with demanding fervency and she answered eagerly, quickly. Finally he drew back. "You'll stay here tonight, just to play safe," he said.

The female in her rose up at once. "Not to fill in for Jodie," she said crossly. "I told you I'm not interested in that."

"Damn if you're not a sassy little thing," Peter said, holding her at arm's length. "I was telling you the truth about why I spent that night here with Jodie. I hoped to get her to reveal something." He paused a moment. "And not what you're thinking," he added, seeing her eyes flash.

"It didn't work," he said. "In fact, I came to realize that Jodie was mostly out to make certain I didn't get to know too much about you and your movements."

"And when you went into Wolf Hollow you were trying to find the old house, weren't you?" Nancy asked.

"Yes, to see for myself," Peter admitted. "I hadn't had a chance then to check out all the dates. That's when I decided I had to get to Louisville to do some on the spot and long-distance checking."

Nancy suddenly was yanked forward into his arms again. "I don't want a replacement for Jodie, not for tonight, or next month, or next year," he said. "I want you, permanently." His lips were on hers again and she was answering. She finally fell asleep in the hollow of his shoulder, the almost-new feeling of being safe hers once again.

# CHAPTER TEN

THE MORNING SUN WAS HOT AND BRILLIANT, and the lush valley was a peaceful, inviting place. It seemed so, anyway, Nancy marveled. She went with Peter to the town beyond Deepwell where the State Police had a barracks. Arrangements were made to pick up Cassie and the railroad conductor in his cave hideaway. The story that Peter told the police would be more interesting as history than anything else, Nancy realized. It was over, the generations of masquerade, and there was really no one left to continue it.

"What will happen to Bloodroots, now?" she asked Peter as they drove back to the cabin.

"It may be taken over by a valley clan," he said. "Or just fall away by itself."

"And Deepwell Valley will go on just as it is, turned in on itself," Nancy added.

"Maybe new blood will come into it, though I doubt it," Peter said. "Places like Deepwell, whether they're in the mountains of Sicily or the Little Smokies of Kentucky, defy the laws of genetics by existing as they do. We learn more every day about new elements in our biological composition. Perhaps one day biologists will come to Deepwell to study these people in a new light. Perhaps they'll learn that the things we call joy, hate, peace, stubbornness, courage, all those things of the mind and heart, can have a physiological influence. Perhaps they'll learn that deep emotional make-up can change the character of chromosomes. Perhaps there are bloodroots, working in ways we have yet to understand."

The car halted before the cabin, and she helped Peter pack his tapes in boxes and load the entire rear seat of the little old Ford. The police had said they'd pick up her bags at the manor house and bring them to the barracks. She was leaving here with Peter for a new life, a happiness she had once despaired of ever finding again. But as Peter got behind the wheel, she stopped suddenly.

"Jed," she said. "I want to see him again, just for a moment, Peter."

"Get in," Peter said gently. "It's up to Jed. He'll find you if he wants to. He has his own ways, you've learned that by now."

"Yes," Nancy said. Jed had his ways, those of a shy boy and an old man full of secret wisdom, the ways of the wanderer and the ways of the rooted, of now and forever. Of all the memories of the Little Smokies, Jed would be the fondest. Peter drove slowly down the road as it narrowed. They'd just turned a bend when she saw the slender figure sitting cross-legged on the rock just over the road, the thatch of blond hair brilliant in the sun. She heard the guitar chord and then the silver, sweet sound of his voice drift down to her.

*"The time it is short, there is none I can spare,*
  *And the nightingale's song will soon die in the air,*
*Don't you think, dearest Nancy, you'd better agree,*
  *To make love while the nightingale sings in the tree,*
*Don't you think, dearest Nancy, you'd better agree,*
  *To make love while the nightingale sings in the tree...."*

Peter's hand closed over hers. "I agree," she said softly. The car rolled on and she waved a hand at the figure on the rock. He didn't wave back but she could see the little elfin smile playing around his lips, and then he was out of sight. She snuggled against Peter and the smile edging her lips was very much the same, full of the wisdom of love.